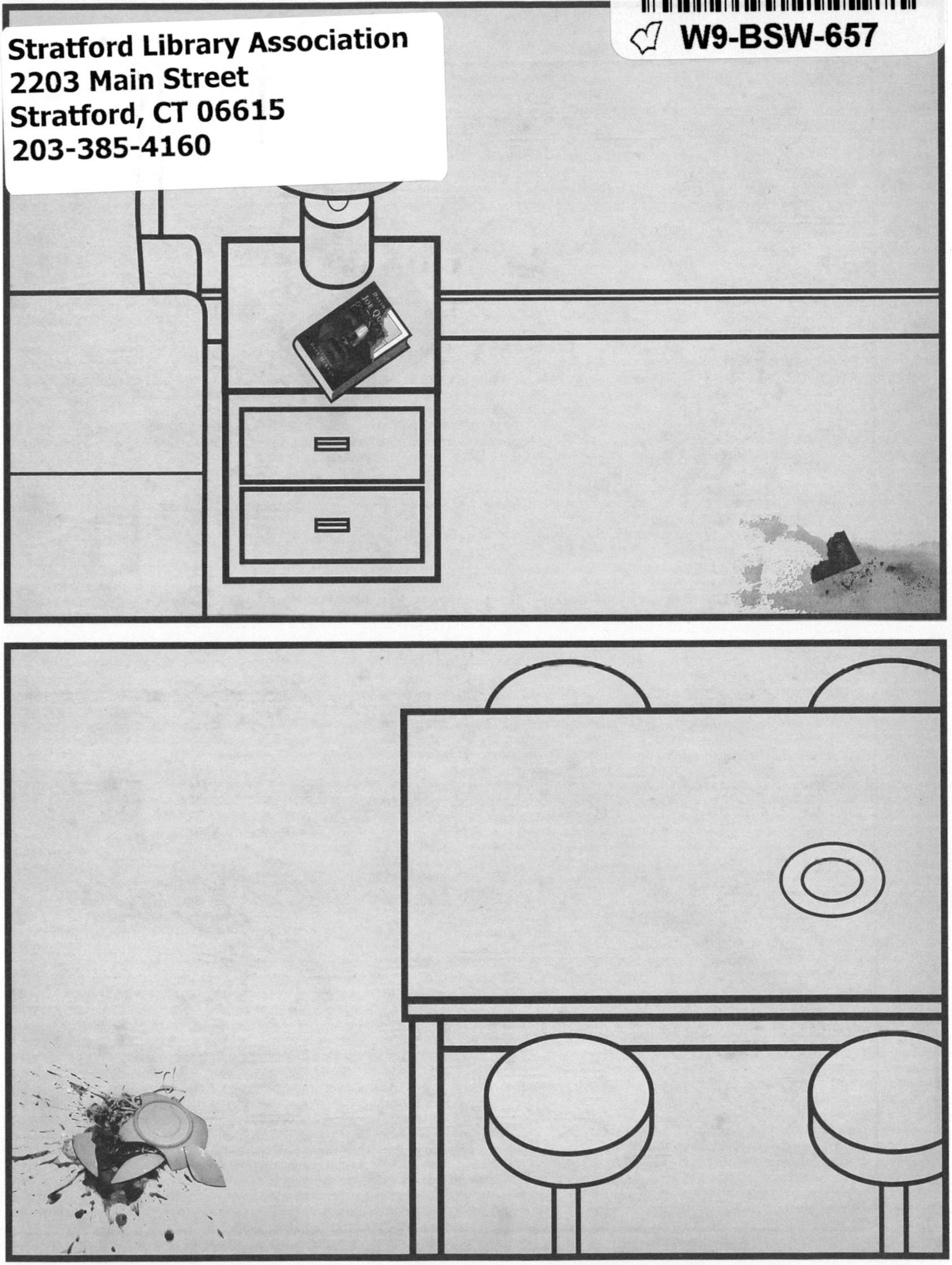

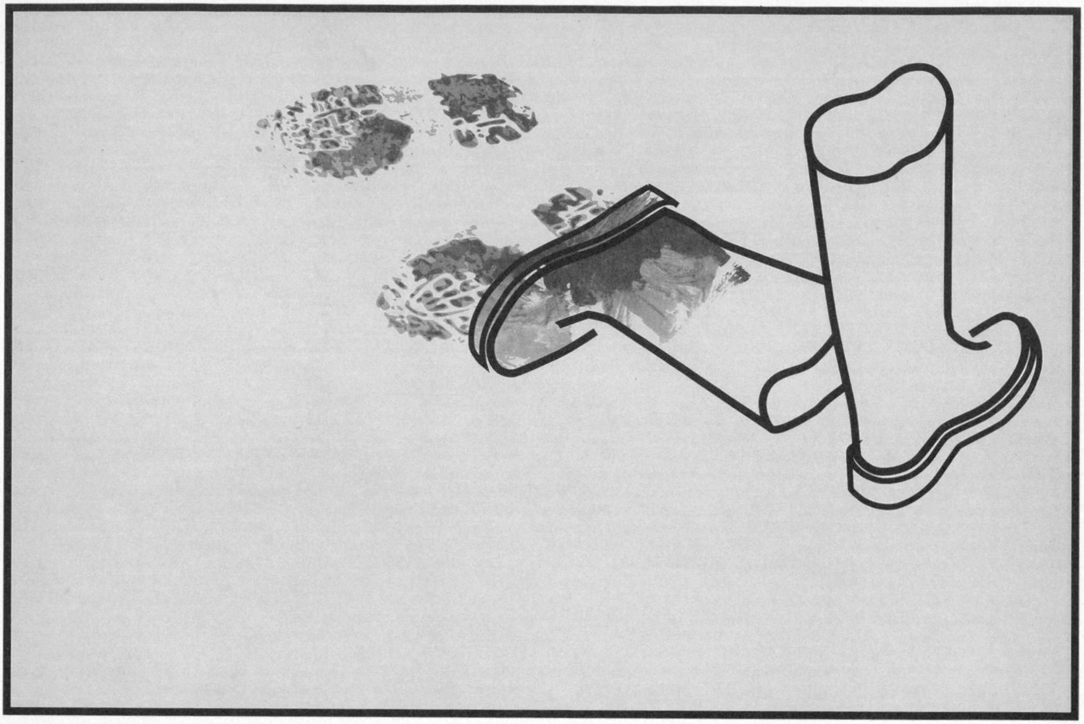
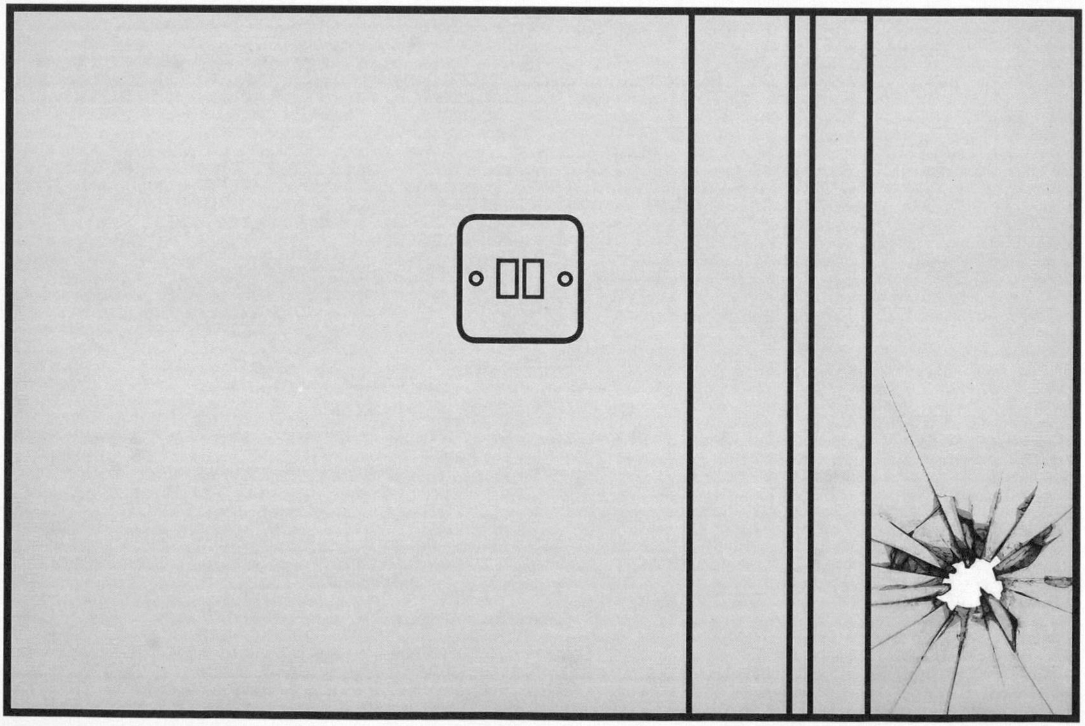

DAVID ALMOND

JOE QUINN'S POLTERGEIST

ILLUSTRATED BY

DAVE MCKEAN

CANDLEWICK PRESS

INTRODUCTION

The library was a couple of streets away from my home: a small branch library, the kind of place we all take for granted, the kind of place that wrong-headed people say has outlived its time. It was close to Felling Square and the Victoria Jubilee pub, where folk gathered around the piano in a side room to sing old songs and tell old tales. And it was just across the street from a patch of grass where I played football as a boy. On one side of the road, as I ran around with Peter, Kev, Colin, and Tex, I imagined being a famous footballer. On the other, I dreamed of being a published author. I'd often go into the library at dusk, when we couldn't see the ball anymore.

I loved the library's Religion and Philosophy section, skimming past the books about worthy saints and famous thinkers and seeking the crazier books, to plunder them for information about ghosts and spirits, clairvoyance, spontaneous combustion, levitation, spirit writing, human vanishings — and poltergeists.

I was also a fan of Hammer horror films, of TV's *The Twilight Zone,* and of Dennis Wheatley's weird and terrifying novels, such as *The Devil Rides Out* and *The Ka of Gifford Hillary*. I loved *The Third Eye* by T. Lobsang Rampa. It told of Lobsang's boyhood in the monasteries and mountains of Tibet, his initiation into ancient mysteries, the operation on his skull that opened up his powers of clairvoyance.

I dreamed of being him. I walked through the streets of Felling trying to feel possessed by him. Then it turned out that Lobsang was Cyril Hoskin, a plumber's son from Devon, and he'd never stepped foot outside the British Isles. But it didn't matter to me. Wasn't that what writers were supposed to do — make things up, make lies seem like truth, create new versions of themselves?

The world was striving to be new. All across Tyneside, the old dark terraced streets were being torn down. Estates in bright new brick and pebbledash, like Leam Lane Estate in this story, were spreading out across the open spaces.

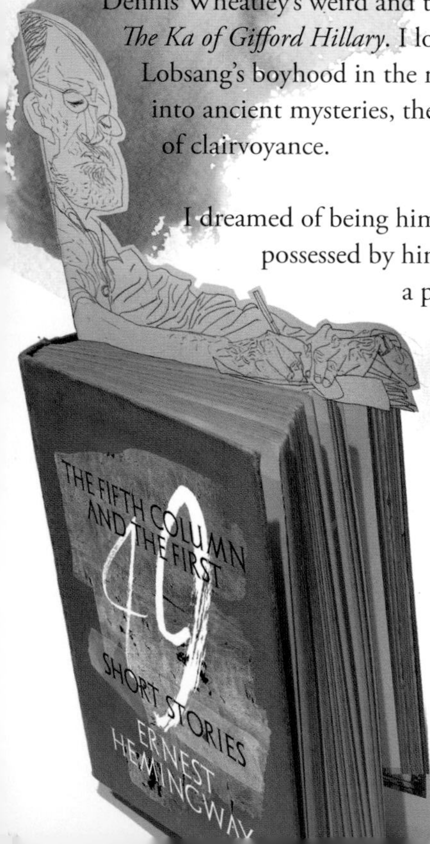
THE FIFTH COLUMN
AND THE FIRST
49
SHORT STORIES
ERNEST
HEMINGWAY

Politicians talked about a world of white-hot technology; we were about to send a man to the moon; *Tomorrow's World* on the BBC told us about cures for cancer, driverless cars, paper pants, self-cleaning clothes, giant carrots, robots, laser beams, jet packs. What a future was to come!

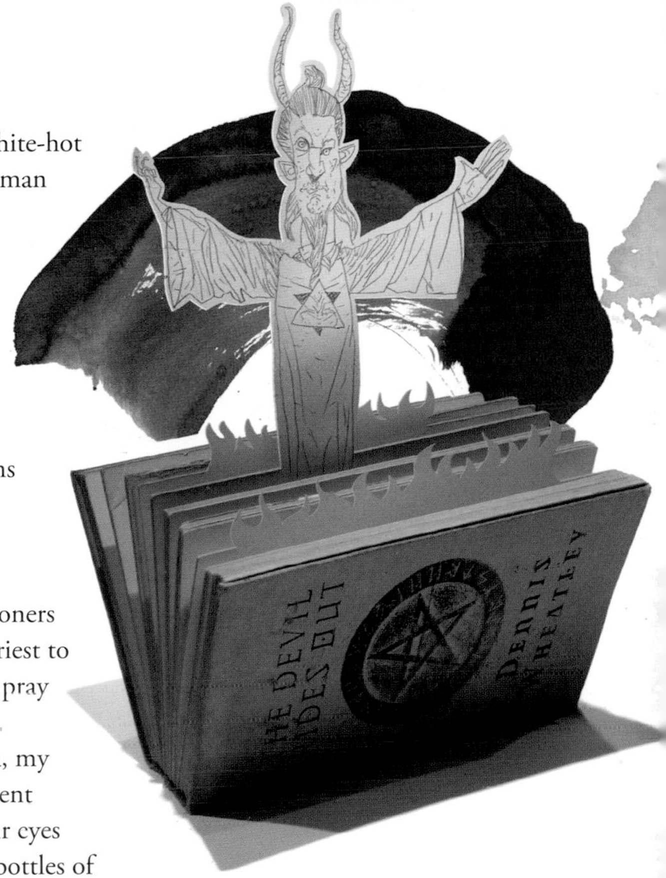
HE DEVIL
IDES OUT
DENNIS
HEATLEY

But the past, and ancient superstitions and religious beliefs, kept reasserting themselves. St. Patrick's Church was packed with people of all ages. Every year a planeful of St. Patrick's parishioners flew to Lourdes in France with the priest to see the miracles and healings, and to pray to Our Lady to be healed themselves. Many of my relatives — my grandma, my uncle Maurice, my auntie Anne — went on these trips. They came home, their eyes shining, carrying Our Lady–shaped bottles of holy water that we used along with medicines to treat coughs and colds, and much more serious diseases.

Tales and rumors showed how difficult it was for some folk to adjust to the new world. They kept ponies in their brand-new dining rooms and chickens on their balconies. Old women read each other's tea leaves in Dragone's. There were tales of ghosts and hauntings in the brightly lit brick and pebbledashed homes. As in the story of Joe Quinn and his poltergeist, a film crew did try to record the ghosts that walked at night and terrified a family in a brand-new house on Leam Lane Estate.

And, of course, despite the hopes inspired by some of the speakers on *Tomorrow's World,* death and sickness didn't go away. Despite modern medicine and surgery, Lourdes water and prayer, I lost my dad to cancer when I was fifteen. And just like Davie, the narrator of the story, I lost a sister, too. Barbara was only a year old when she died; I was seven.

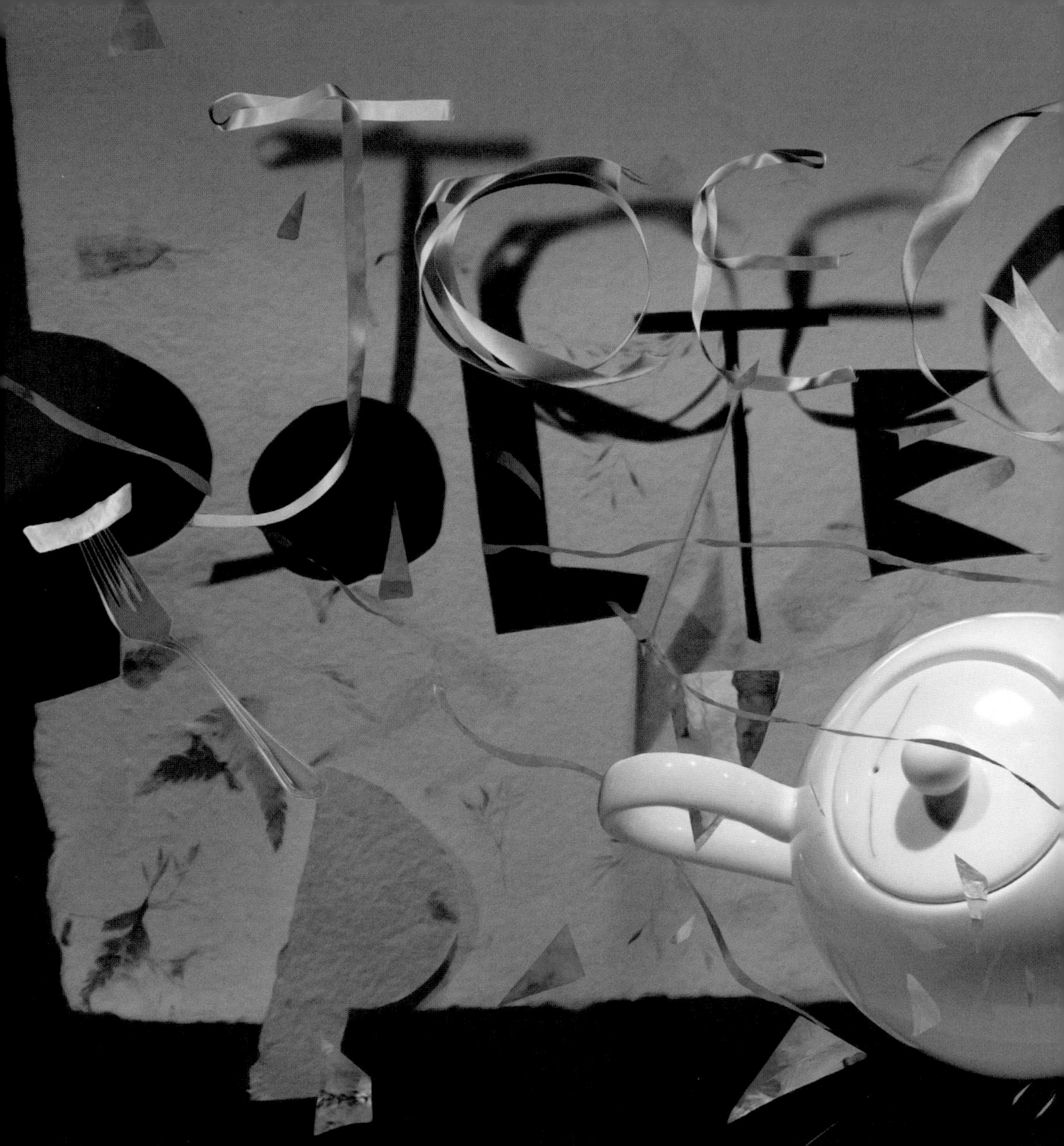

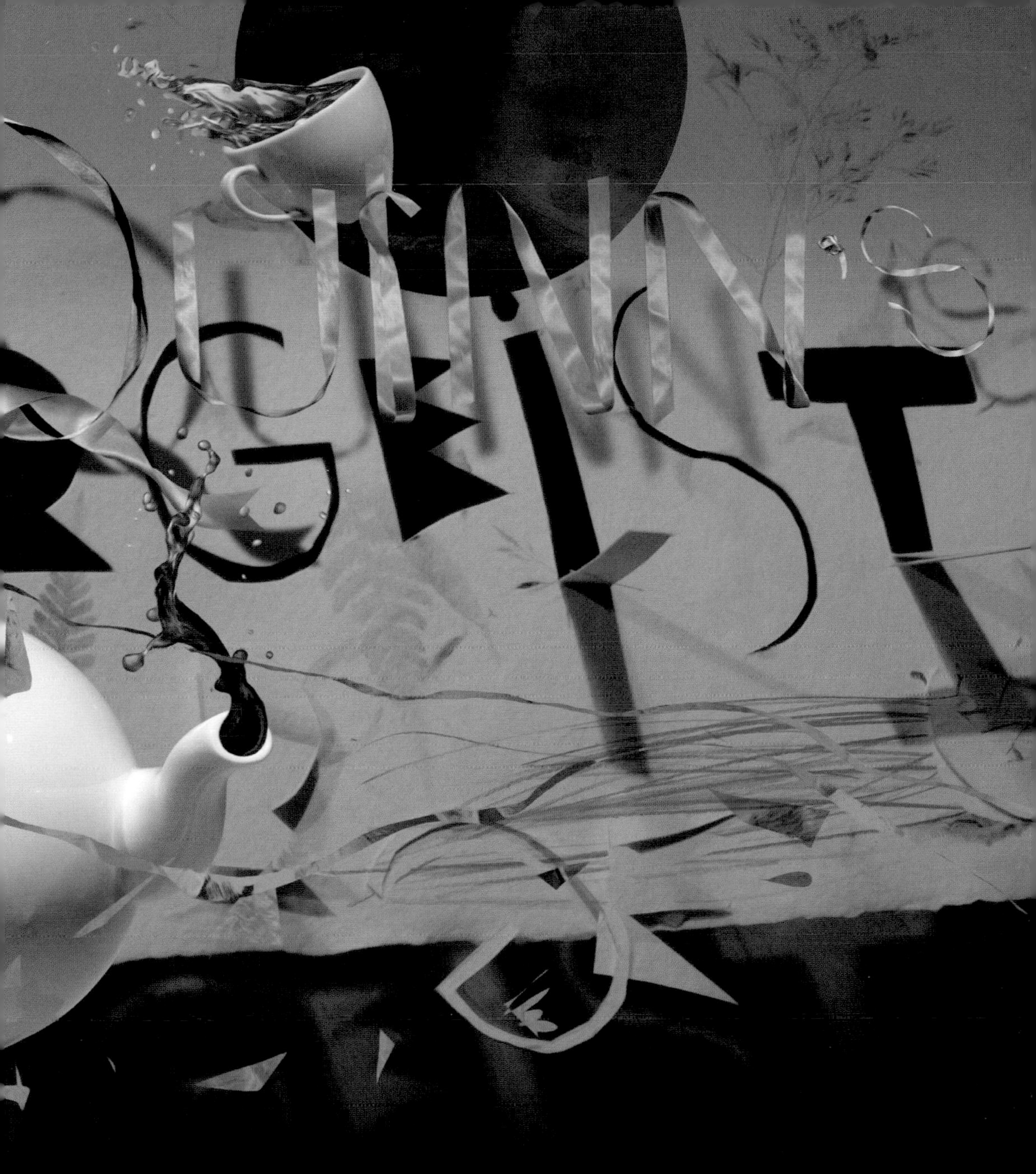

Text previously published in the U.S. in 2015 in *Half a Creature From the Sea: A Life in Stories* under ISBN 978-0-7636-7877-7
Library of Congress Catalog Card Number pending. ISBN 978-1-5362-0160-4
19 20 21 22 23 24 LEO 10 9 8 7 6 5 4 3 2 1
Printed in Heshan, Guangdong, China
This book was typeset in Aunt Mildred. The illustrations were done in mixed media.
Candlewick Press, 99 Dover Street, Somerville, Massachusetts 02144
visit us at www.candlewick.com

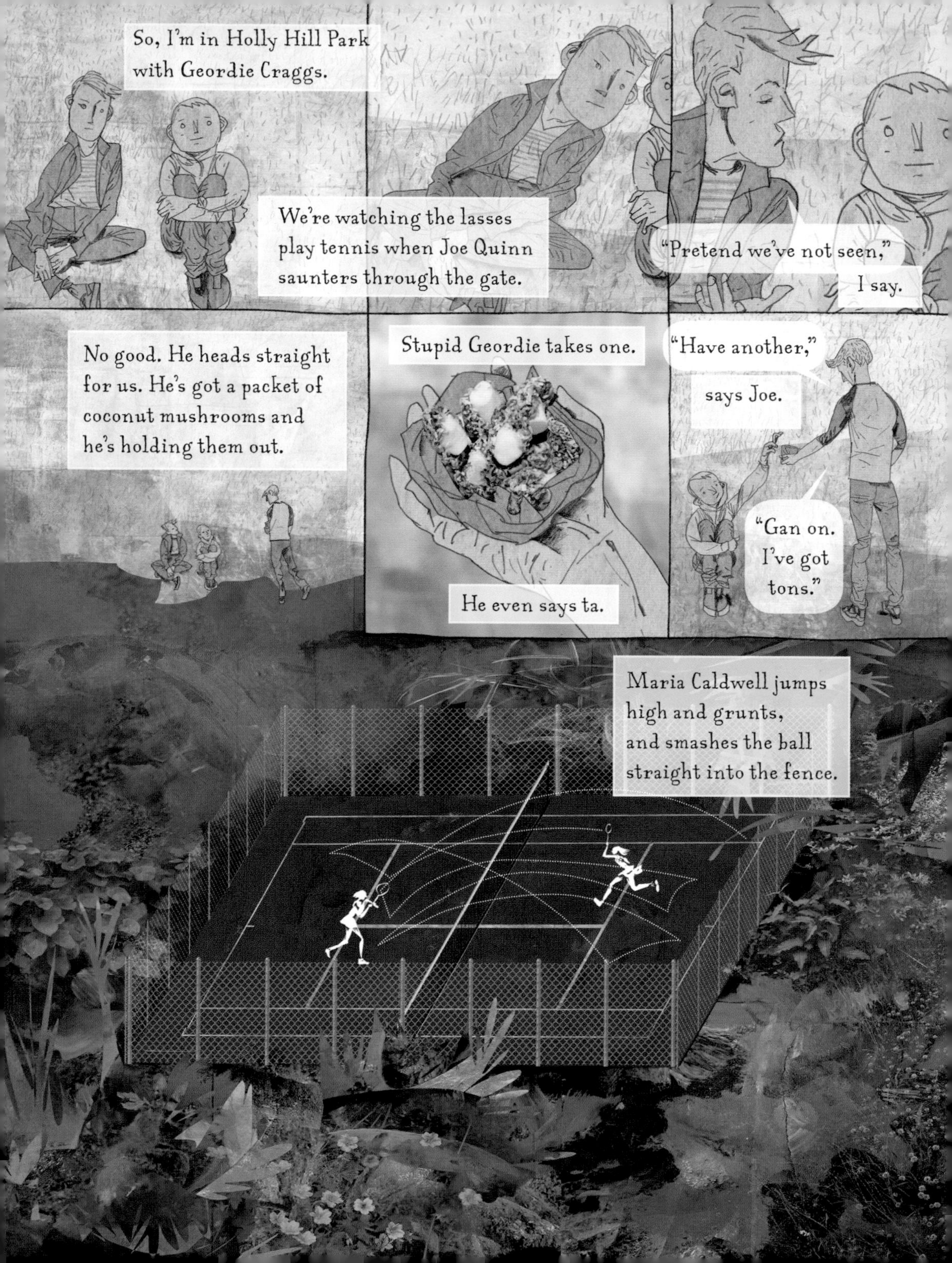
So, I'm in Holly Hill Park with Geordie Craggs.
We're watching the lasses play tennis when Joe Quinn saunters through the gate.
"Pretend we've not seen," I say.
No good. He heads straight for us. He's got a packet of coconut mushrooms and he's holding them out.
Stupid Geordie takes one.
He even says ta.
"Have another," says Joe.
"Gan on. I've got tons."
Maria Caldwell jumps high and grunts, and smashes the ball straight into the fence.

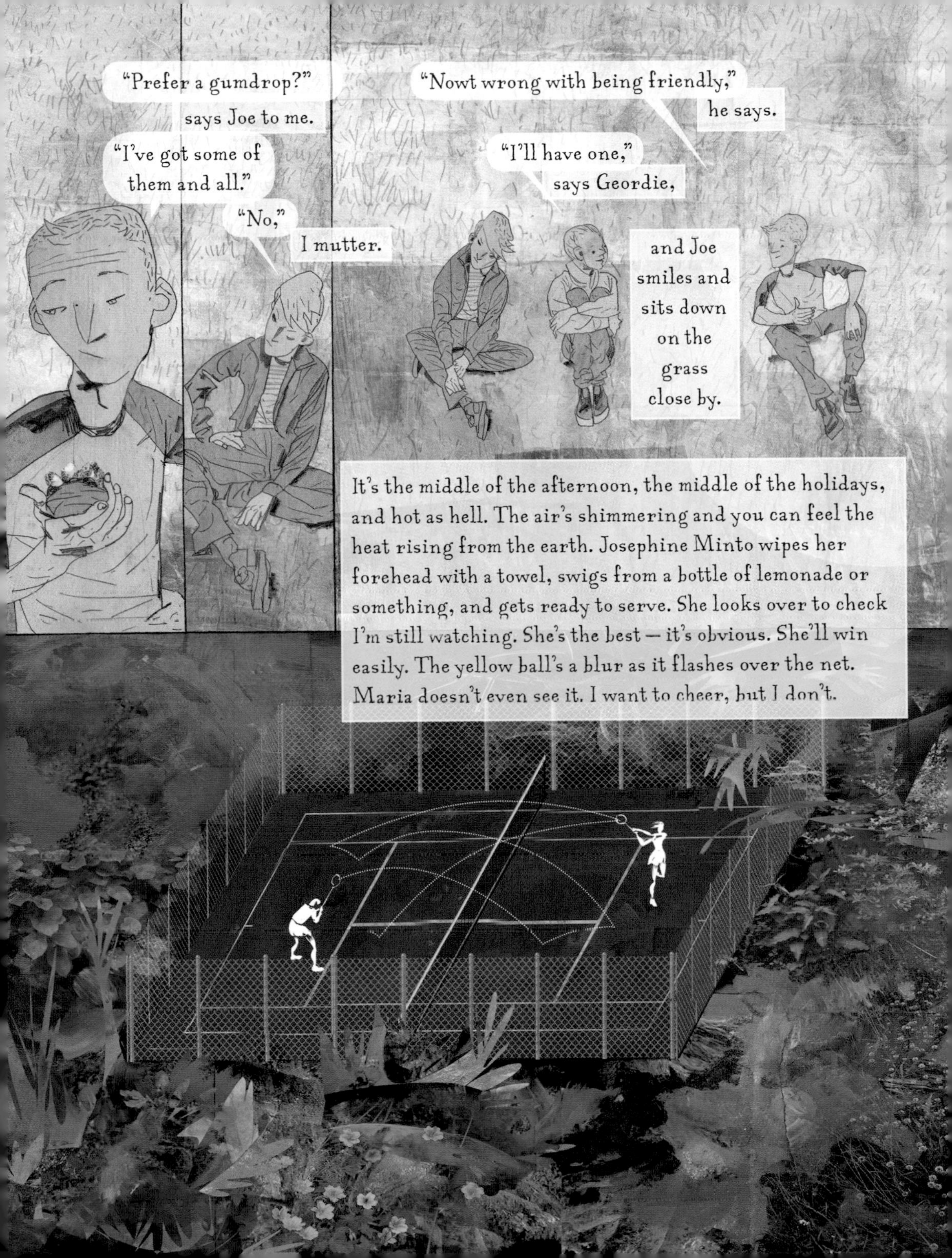
"Prefer a gumdrop?"
says Joe to me.
"I've got some of them and all."
"No,"
I mutter.
"Nowt wrong with being friendly,"
he says.
"I'll have one,"
says Geordie,
and Joe smiles and sits down on the grass close by.
It's the middle of the afternoon, the middle of the holidays, and hot as hell. The air's shimmering and you can feel the heat rising from the earth. Josephine Minto wipes her forehead with a towel, swigs from a bottle of lemonade or something, and gets ready to serve. She looks over to check I'm still watching. She's the best — it's obvious. She'll win easily. The yellow ball's a blur as it flashes over the net. Maria doesn't even see it. I want to cheer, but I don't.

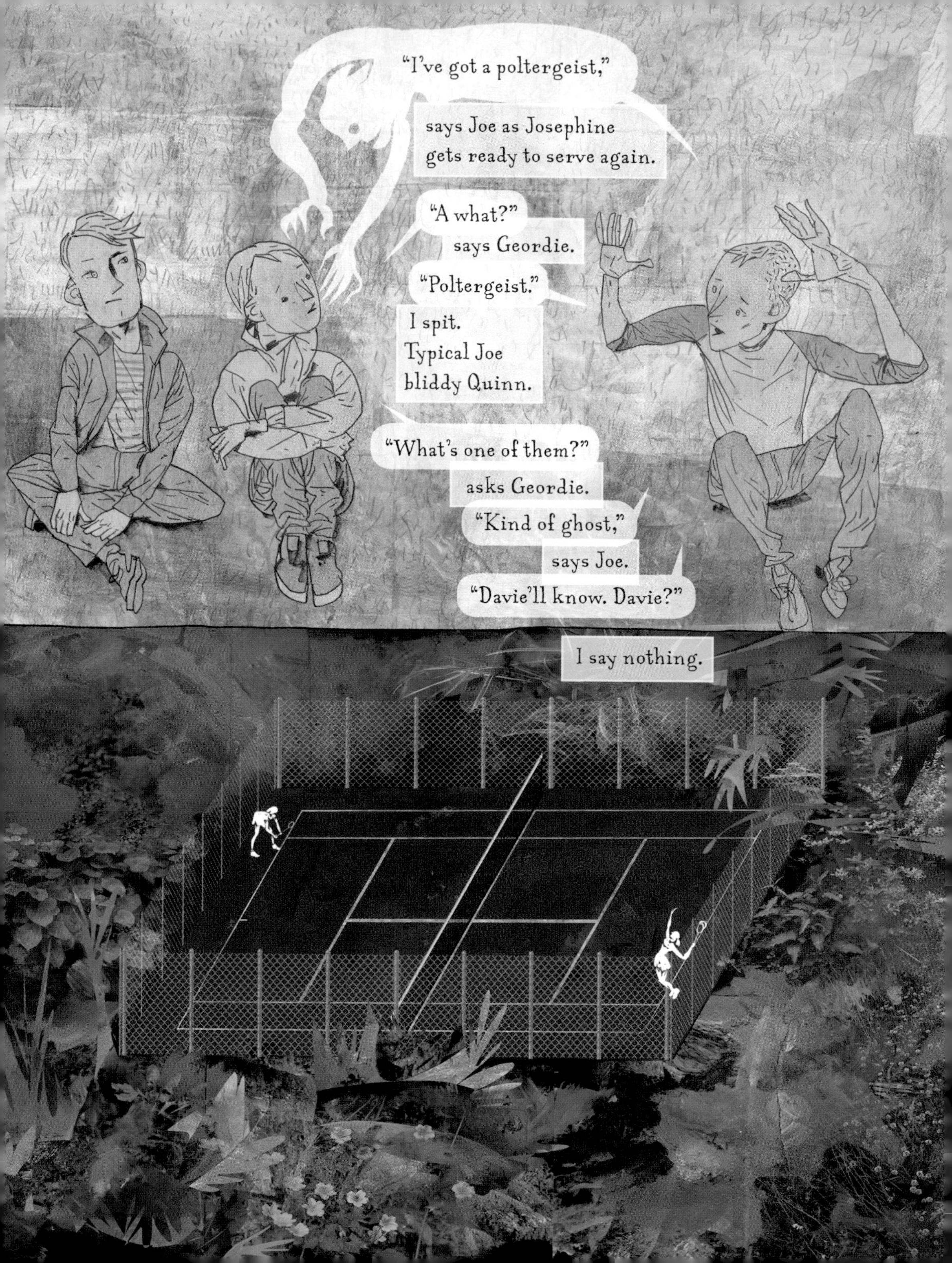
"I've got a poltergeist,"
says Joe as Josephine gets ready to serve again.
"A what?"
says Geordie.
"Poltergeist."
I spit. Typical Joe bliddy Quinn.
"What's one of them?"
asks Geordie.
"Kind of ghost,"
says Joe.
"Davie'll know. Davie?"
I say nothing.

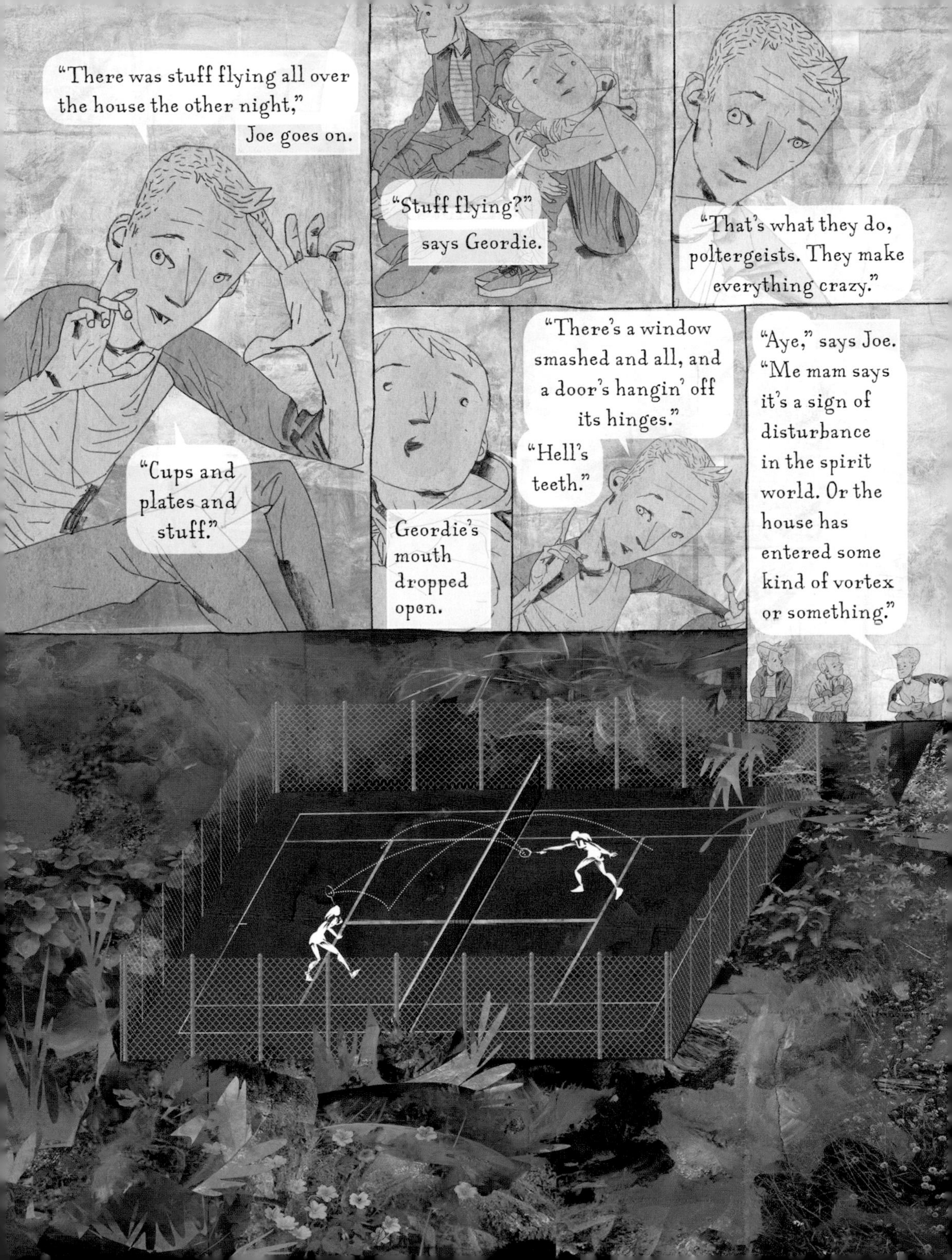
"There was stuff flying all over the house the other night,"
Joe goes on.
"Cups and plates and stuff."
"Stuff flying?"
says Geordie.
"That's what they do, poltergeists. They make everything crazy."
Geordie's mouth dropped open.
"There's a window smashed and all, and a door's hangin' off its hinges."
"Hell's teeth."
"Aye," says Joe. "Me mam says it's a sign of disturbance in the spirit world. Or the house has entered some kind of vortex or something."

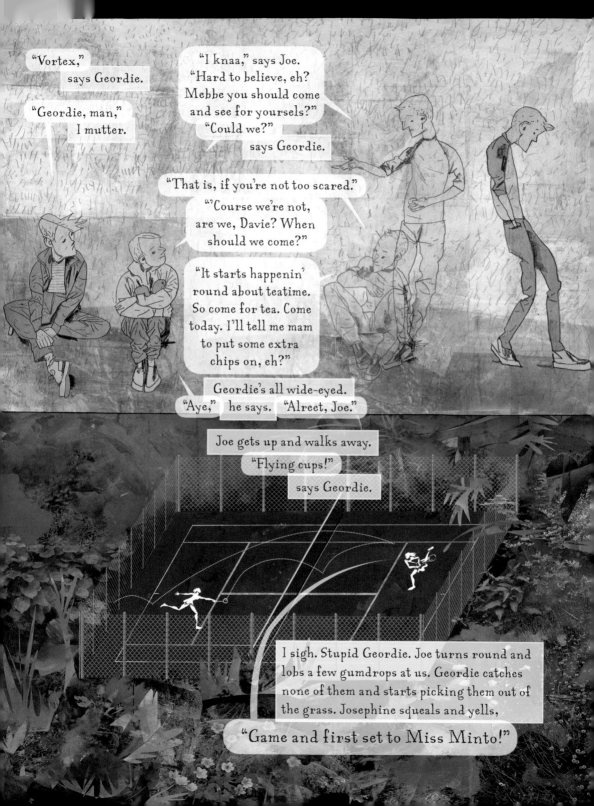

"Vortex," says Geordie.

"Geordie, man," I mutter.

"I knaa," says Joe. "Hard to believe, eh? Mebbe you should come and see for yoursels?" "Could we?" says Geordie.

"That is, if you're not too scared."

"'Course we're not, are we, Davie? When should we come?"

"It starts happenin' round about teatime. So come for tea. Come today. I'll tell me mam to put some extra chips on, eh?"

Geordie's all wide-eyed. "Aye," he says. "Alreet, Joe."

Joe gets up and walks away. "Flying cups!" says Geordie.

I sigh. Stupid Geordie. Joe turns round and lobs a few gumdrops at us. Geordie catches none of them and starts picking them out of the grass. Josephine squeals and yells,

"Game and first set to Miss Minto!"

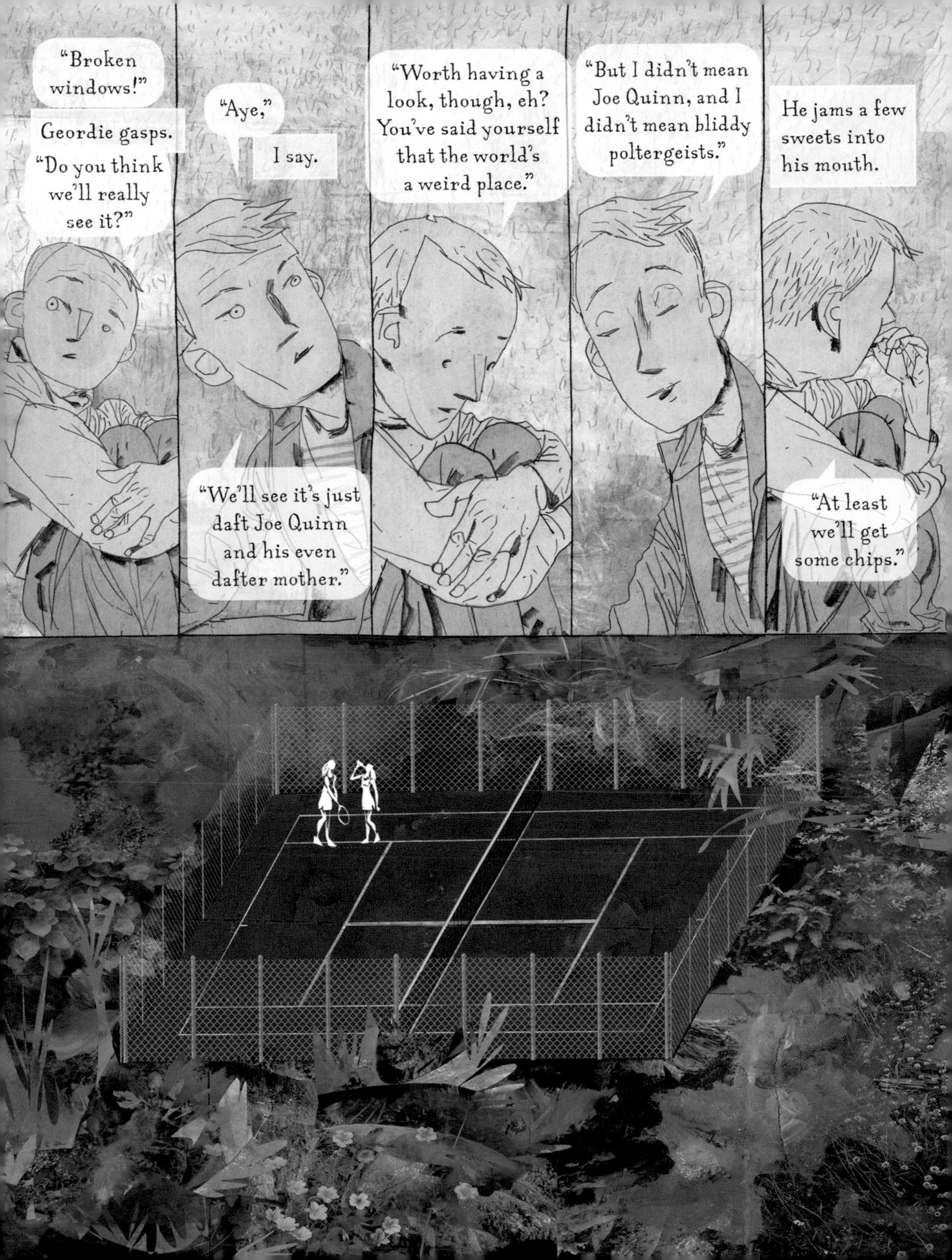
"Broken windows!"
Geordie gasps.
"Do you think we'll really see it?"
"Aye,"
I say.
"We'll see it's just daft Joe Quinn and his even dafter mother."
"Worth having a look, though, eh? You've said yourself that the world's a weird place."
"But I didn't mean Joe Quinn, and I didn't mean bliddy poltergeists."
He jams a few sweets into his mouth.
"At least we'll get some chips."

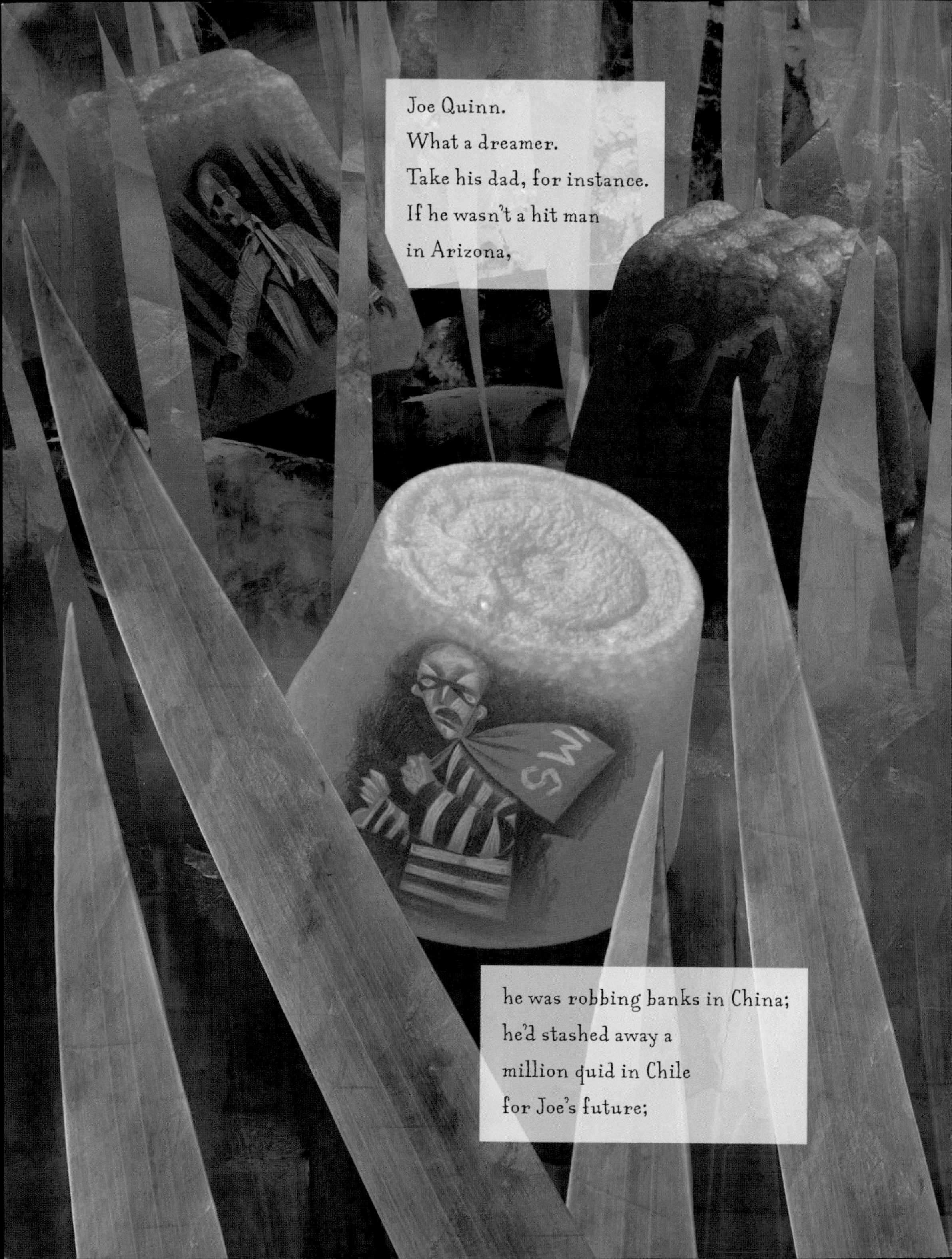

Joe Quinn.
What a dreamer.
Take his dad, for instance.
If he wasn't a hit man
in Arizona,

he was robbing banks in China;
he'd stashed away a
million quid in Chile
for Joe's future;

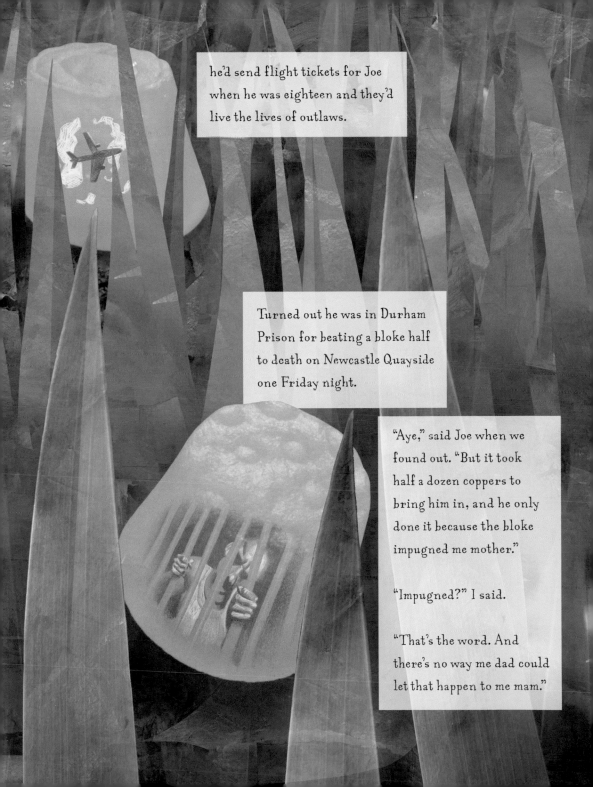

he'd send flight tickets for Joe when he was eighteen and they'd live the lives of outlaws.

Turned out he was in Durham Prison for beating a bloke half to death on Newcastle Quayside one Friday night.

"Aye," said Joe when we found out. "But it took half a dozen coppers to bring him in, and he only done it because the bloke impugned me mother."

"Impugned?" I said.

"That's the word. And there's no way me dad could let that happen to me mam."

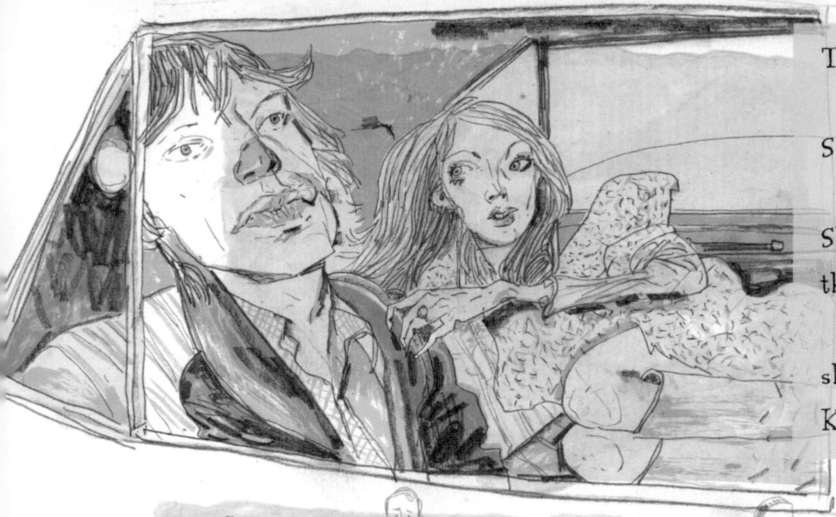

The mother.

She was another one.

She'd been on tours with the Rolling Stones;

she'd danced for the King of Thailand;

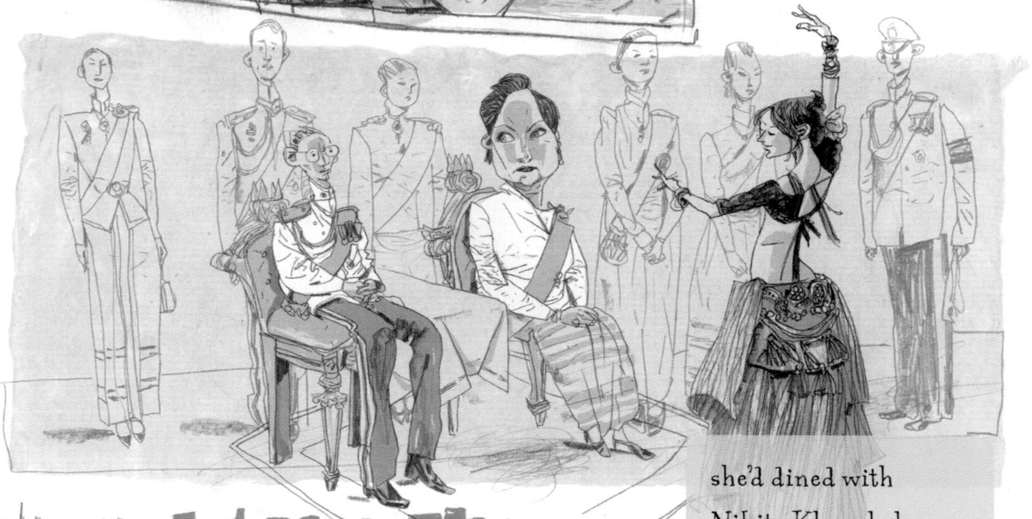

she'd dined with Nikita Khrushchev.

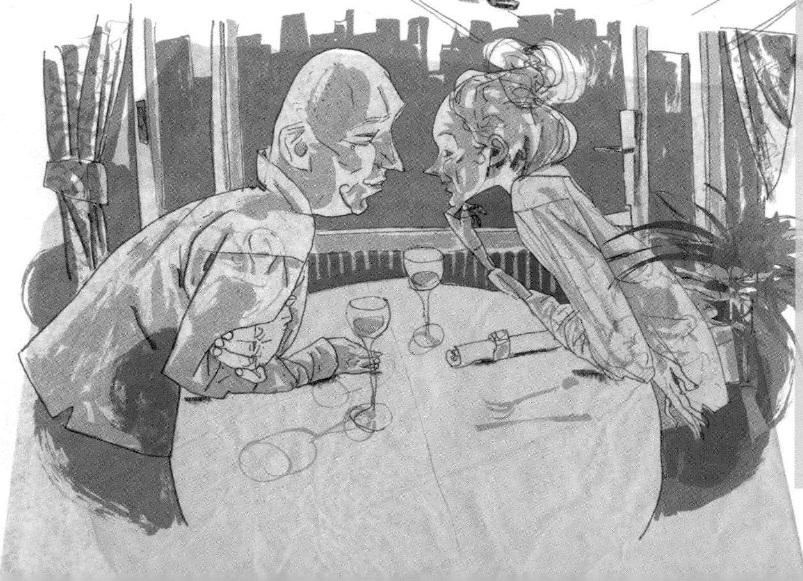

"So what you doing on Leam Lane Estate?" I said.
"It's just till I get some education under me belt. And till me dad gets out. Then she says the world's our oyster."

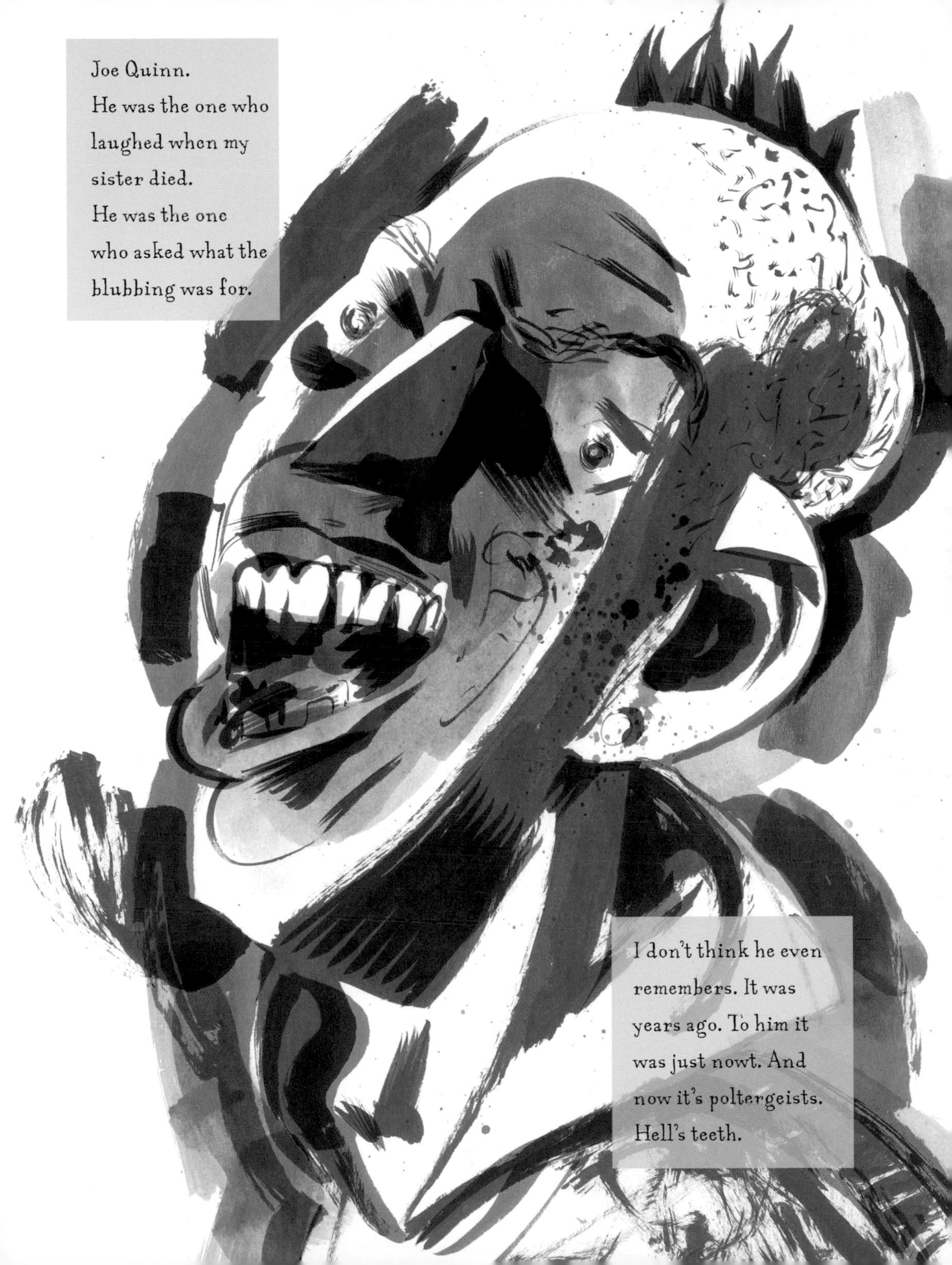

Joe Quinn.
He was the one who laughed when my sister died.
He was the one who asked what the blubbing was for.
I don't think he even remembers. It was years ago. To him it was just nowt. And now it's poltergeists. Hell's teeth.

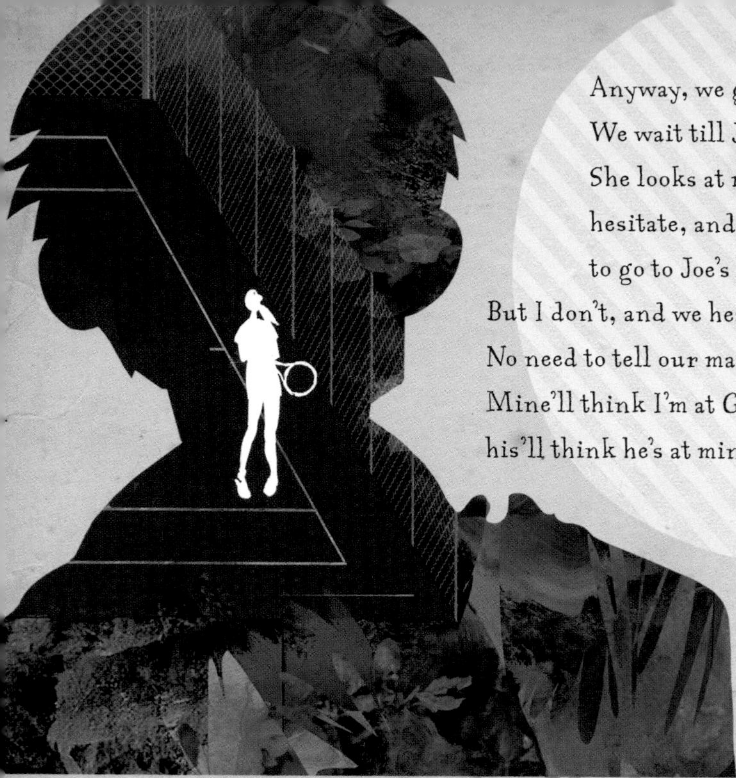

Anyway, we go.
We wait till Josephine's got game, set, and match.
She looks at me and I look at her, and we both
hesitate, and I wonder, should I tell Geordie
to go to Joe's himself?
But I don't, and we head off.
No need to tell our mams.
Mine'll think I'm at Geordie's;
his'll think he's at mine.

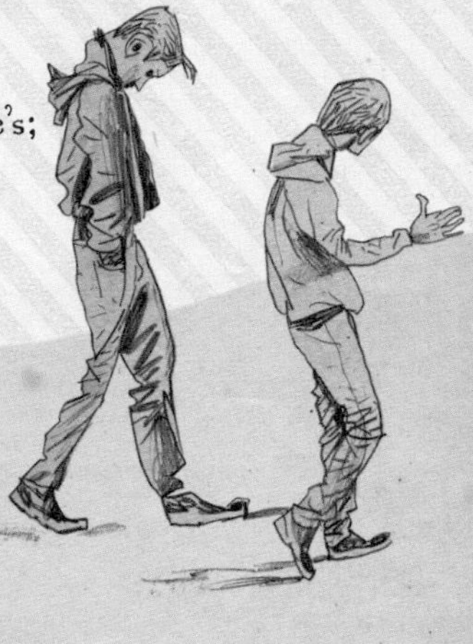

We pass the new priest,
Father Kelly, as we leave the park.
He's standing under a cherry tree,
in his long black robe, smoking.

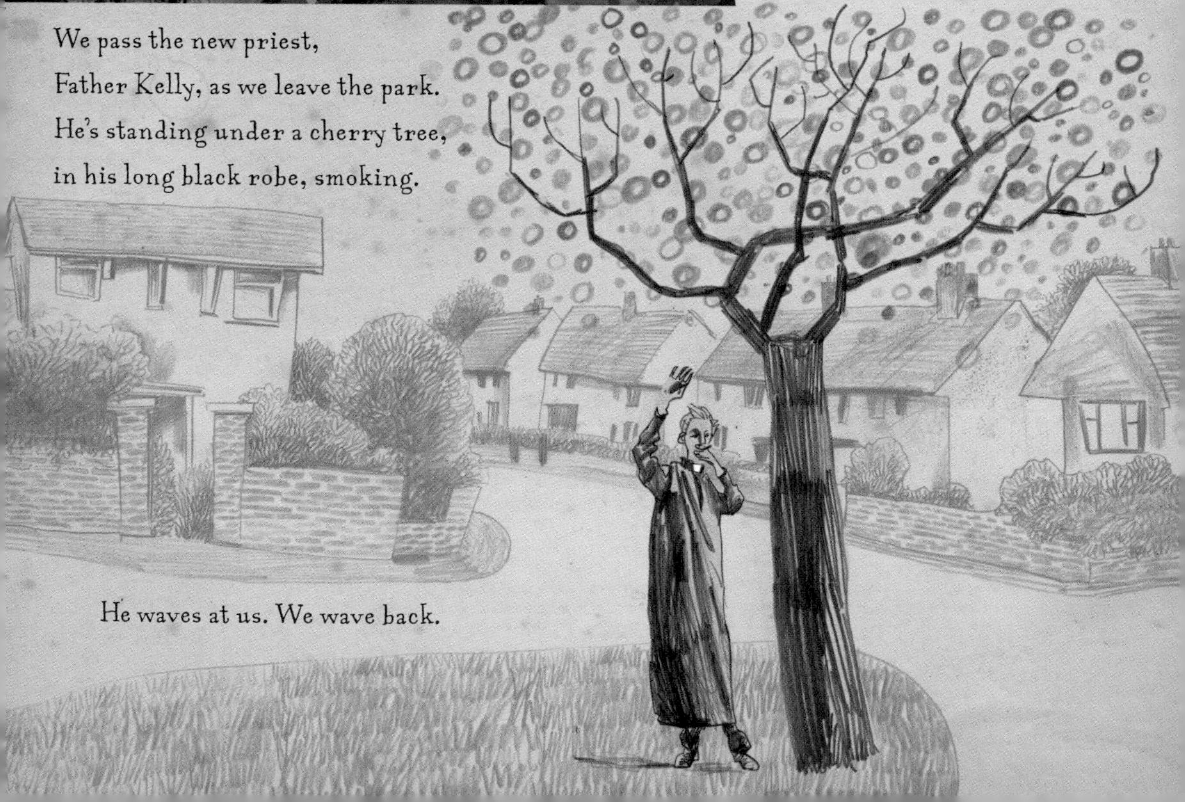

He waves at us. We wave back.

We walk down The Drive.

We're parched, so we stop at Wiffen's and buy some pop.

"We're bliddy daft," I say. "It's a wild goose chase."

"Flying plates, man!" says Geordie. "Smashed windows!"

He starts on about the ghost they had at Wilfie Mack's house a couple
of years back, the one where the telly reporter and the cameraman
stayed all night to watch for it.

"And they saw absolutely nowt," I say.

"Aye, but they said they definitely felt something.
And there was that weird shadow. Remember, Davie?"

I shrug.

"And look what happened to Wilfie just two weeks later."

"Aye," I say finally, and shudder,
despite the baking heat.

We reach the estate and turn into Sullivan Street.

Lots of the front doors are wide open. Some of them have
got stripy plastic curtains dangling, to keep the flies out.

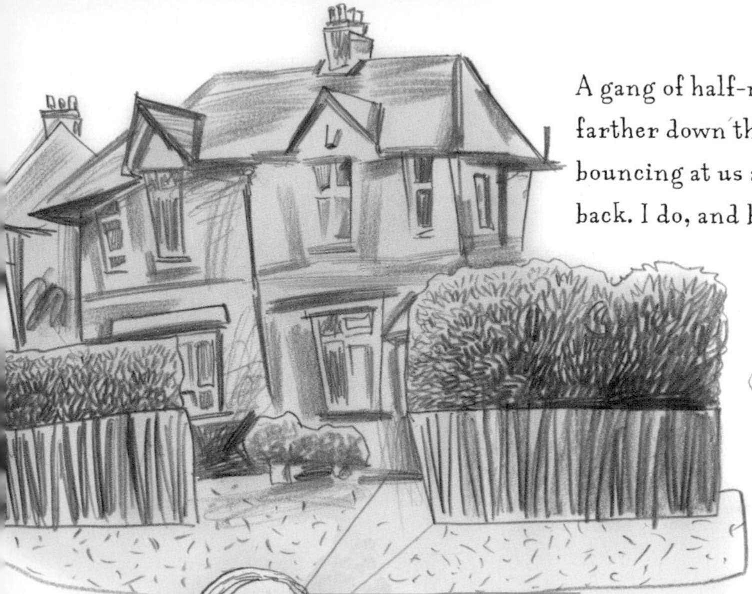

A gang of half-naked kids are playing football farther down the street. Their ball comes bouncing at us and they scream at us to kick it back. I do, and back it flies in a dead straight line.

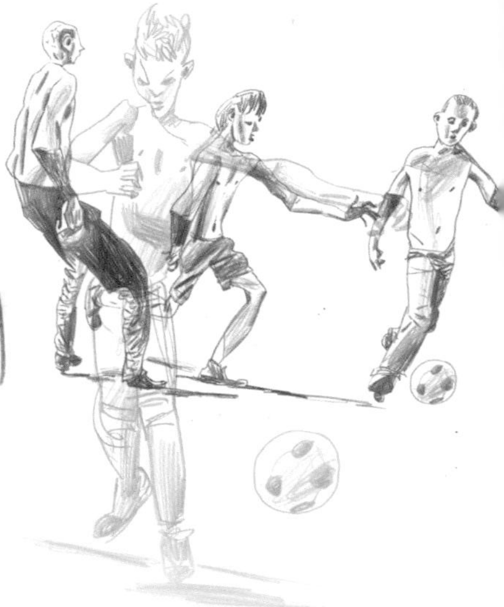

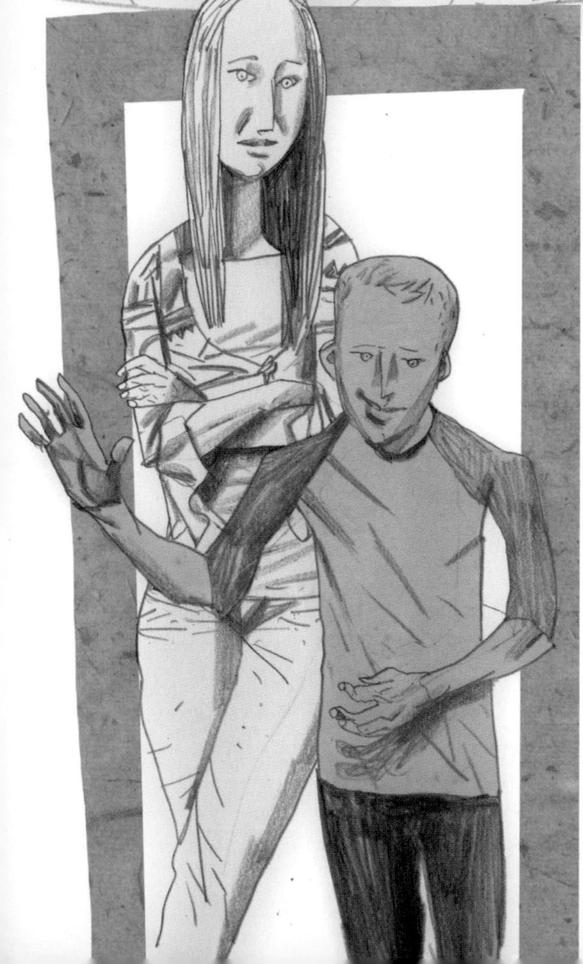

No sign of anybody at Joe's.
The curtains are closed at the front and the door's shut. We head down the side of the house. The back garden's baked mud and clay, hard as stone. It's dead quiet. Then suddenly the back door's wide open and Joe's there, grinning. Mrs. Quinn's behind him with her arms crossed.

"Hello, boys," she says.
"Why don't you step inside?"

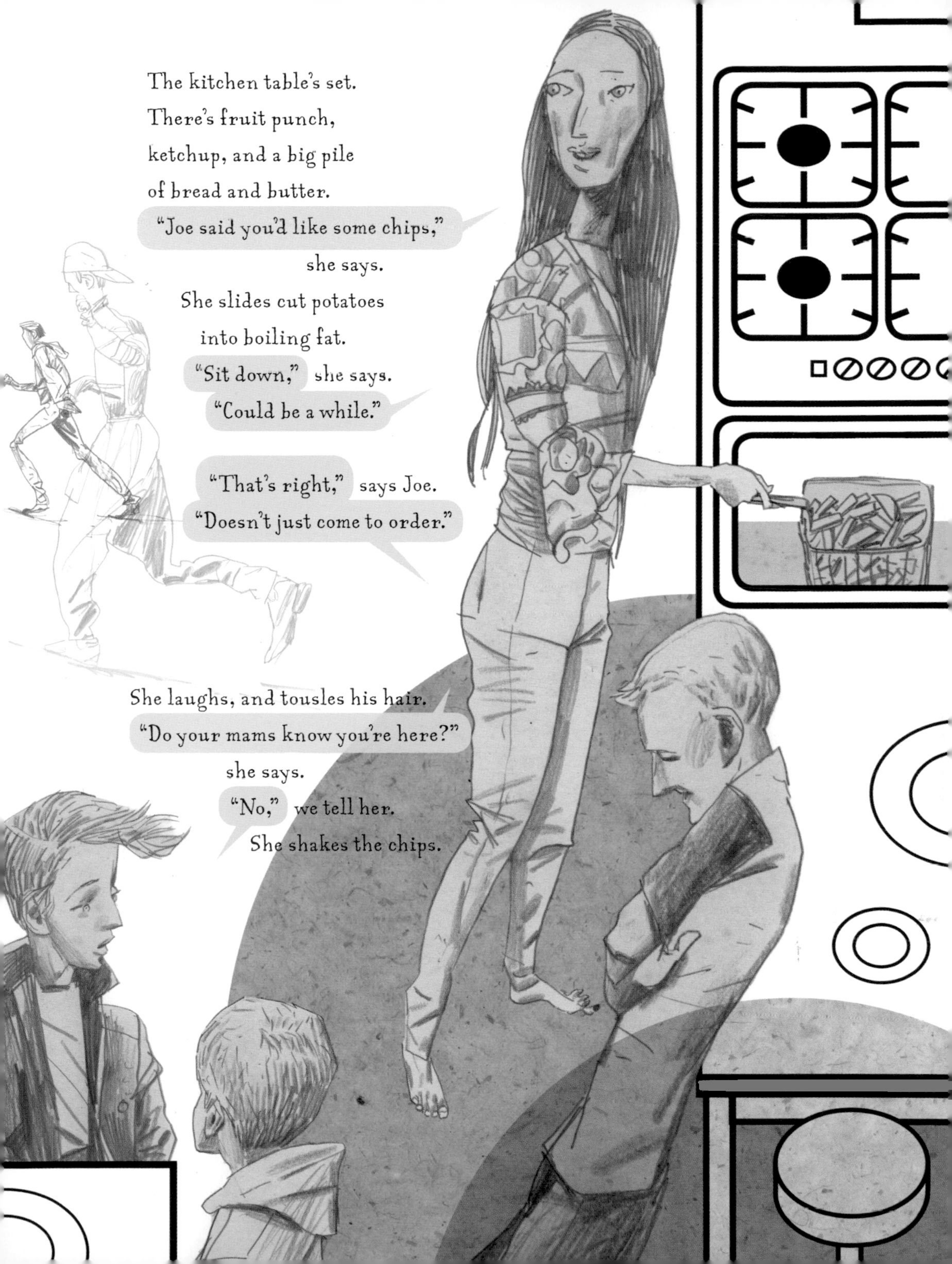

The kitchen table's set.
There's fruit punch,
ketchup, and a big pile
of bread and butter.
"Joe said you'd like some chips,"
she says.
She slides cut potatoes
into boiling fat.
"Sit down," she says.
"Could be a while."

"That's right," says Joe.
"Doesn't just come to order."

She laughs, and tousles his hair.
"Do your mams know you're here?"
she says.
"No," we tell her.
She shakes the chips.

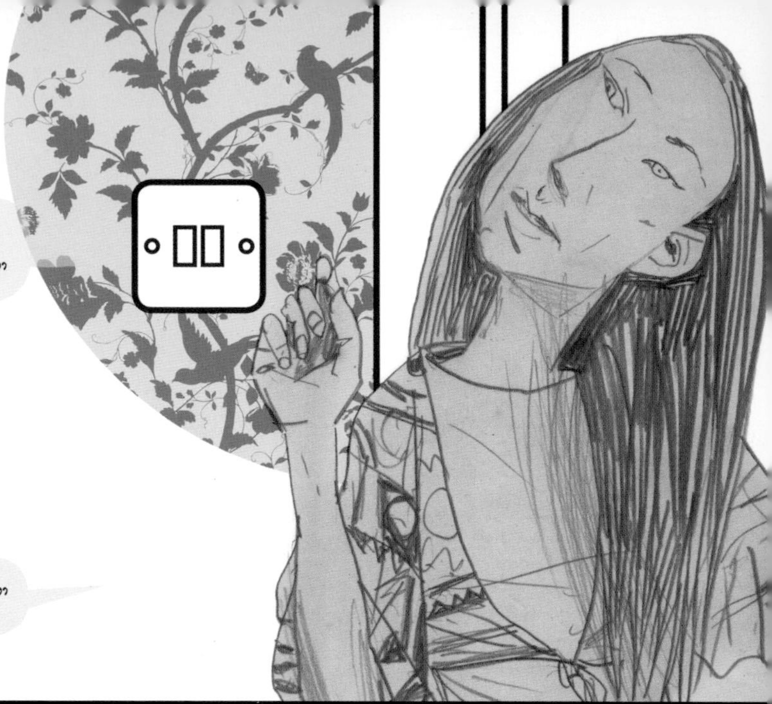

"You're the one whose sister died, aren't you?" she says to me.

I flinch.

"Aye," I say.

"Any sign of her since?"

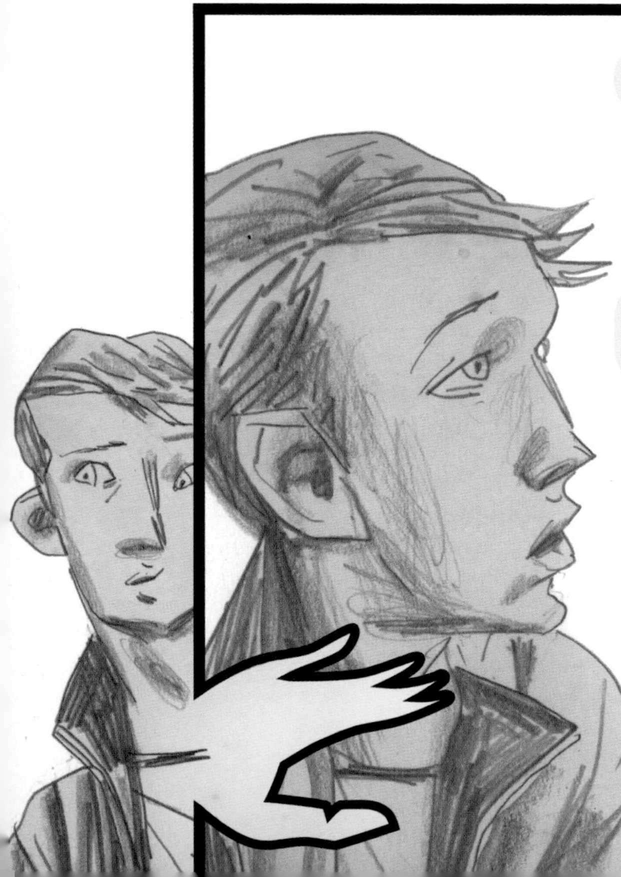

"What?"

She smiles.

"Never mind," she says. "Look. That's the broken window Joe told you about."

It's the narrow pane at the top of the kitchen window. I imagine a knife flying through it, or a fork.

"I should put tape or something over it," she says. "But it's nice to have a bit of breeze in this heat.

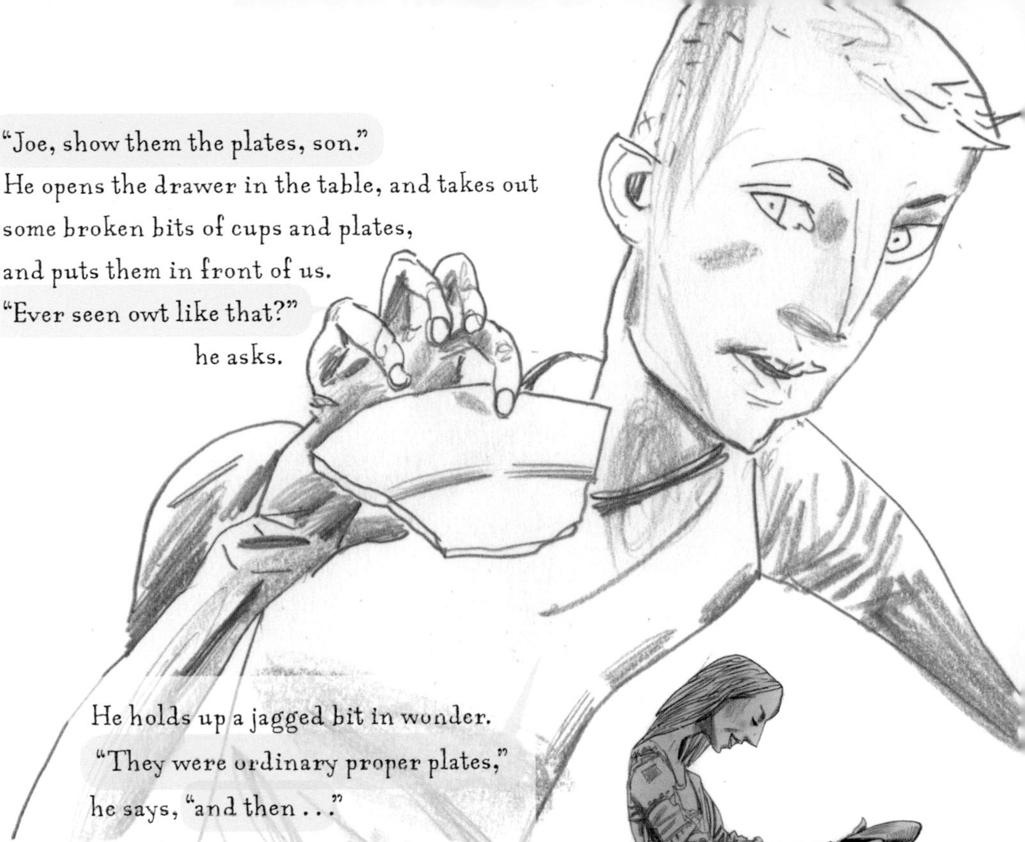

"Joe, show them the plates, son."
He opens the drawer in the table, and takes out
some broken bits of cups and plates,
and puts them in front of us.
"Ever seen owt like that?"
he asks.

He holds up a jagged bit in wonder.
"They were ordinary proper plates,"
he says, "and then . . ."
There's a record player on the
kitchen bench. His mam drops
a record onto the turntable.
A voice and a guitar start wailing.
"You won't have heard this," she tells us.
"They're underground, from California."

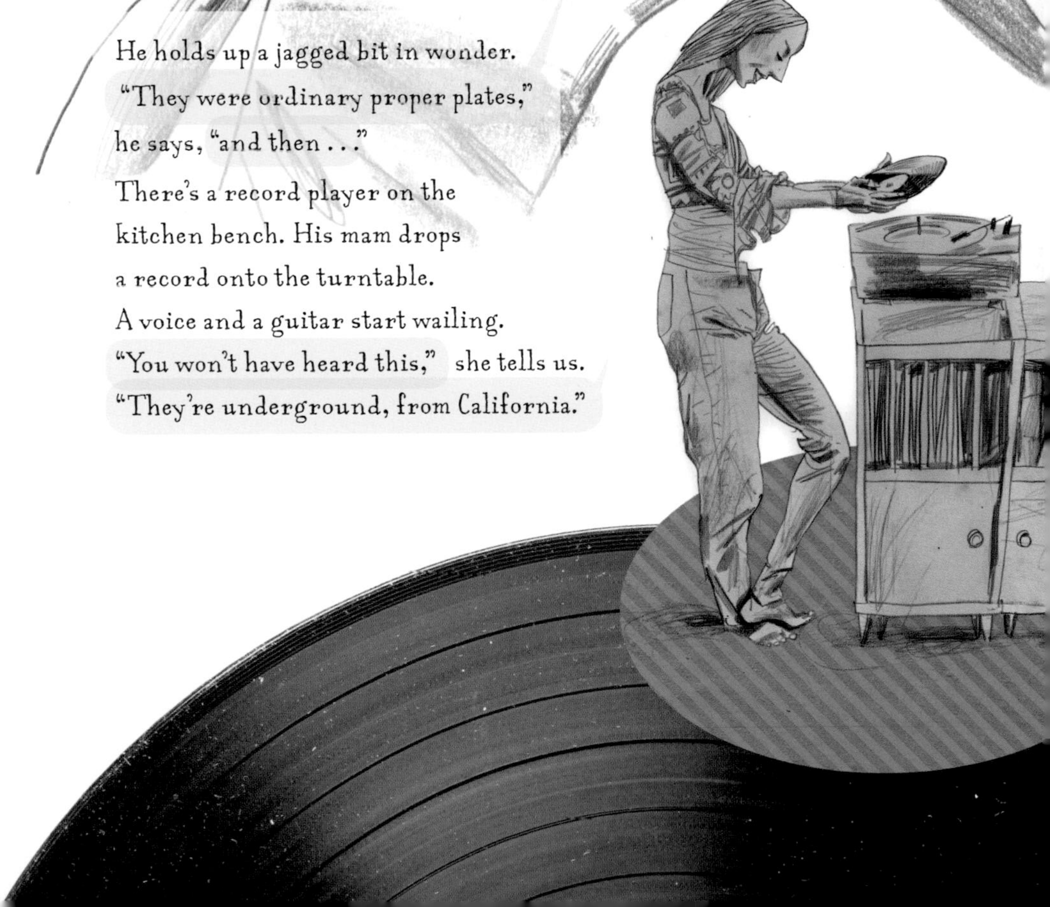

She starts dancing, swinging her arms around her head, and her hair falls back and forward over her shoulders.

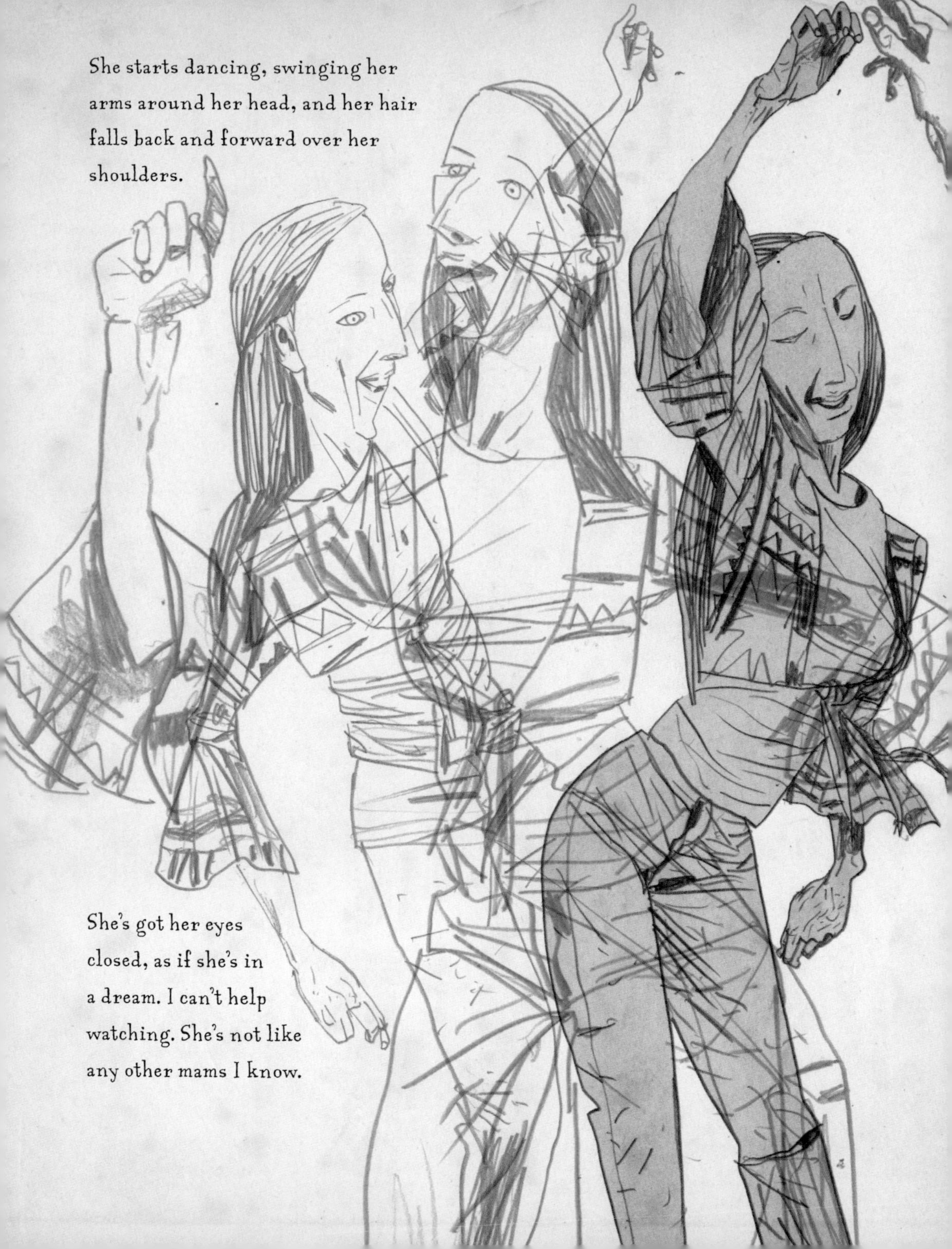

She's got her eyes closed, as if she's in a dream. I can't help watching. She's not like any other mams I know.

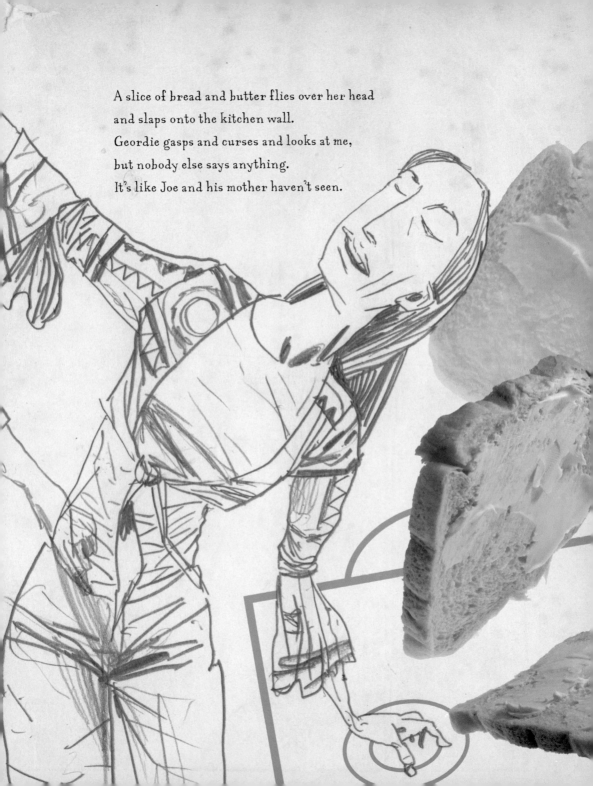

A slice of bread and butter flies over her head
and slaps onto the kitchen wall.
Geordie gasps and curses and looks at me,
but nobody else says anything.
It's like Joe and his mother haven't seen.

Soon the chips are done.
Mrs. Quinn tips them into a bowl,
leans over the table, and puts them
onto our plates.
"Tuck in,"
she says.

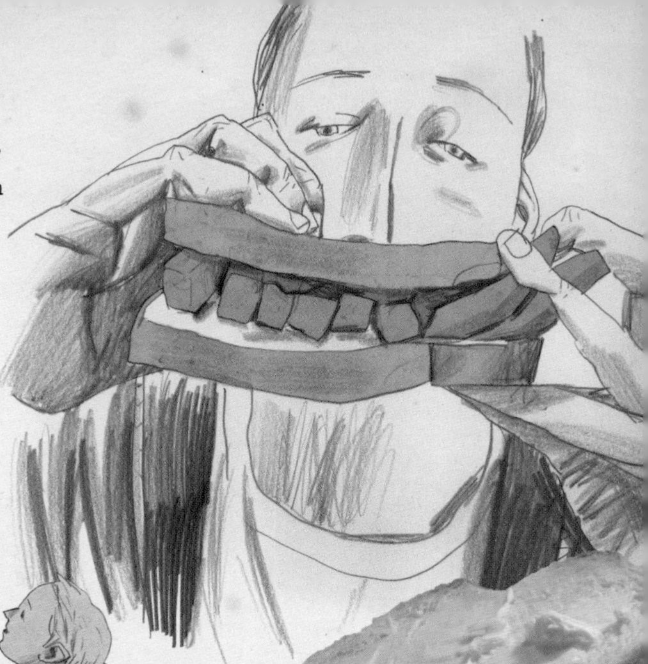

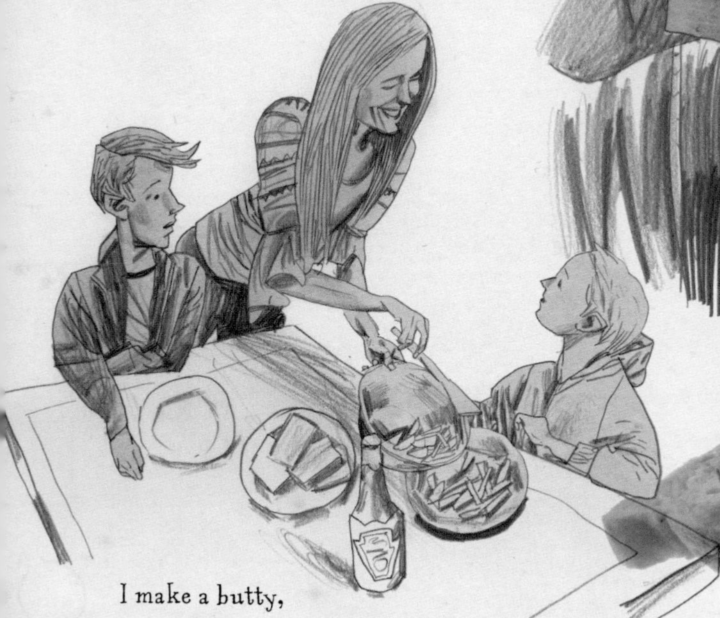

I make a butty,
a layer of chips and ketchup
between two slices of bread.
Lovely.
Then another slice of
bread and butter flies
across the room.
Geordie bursts out laughing.
"That was you!"
he says to Joe.
Joe just shakes his head
and goes on eating.

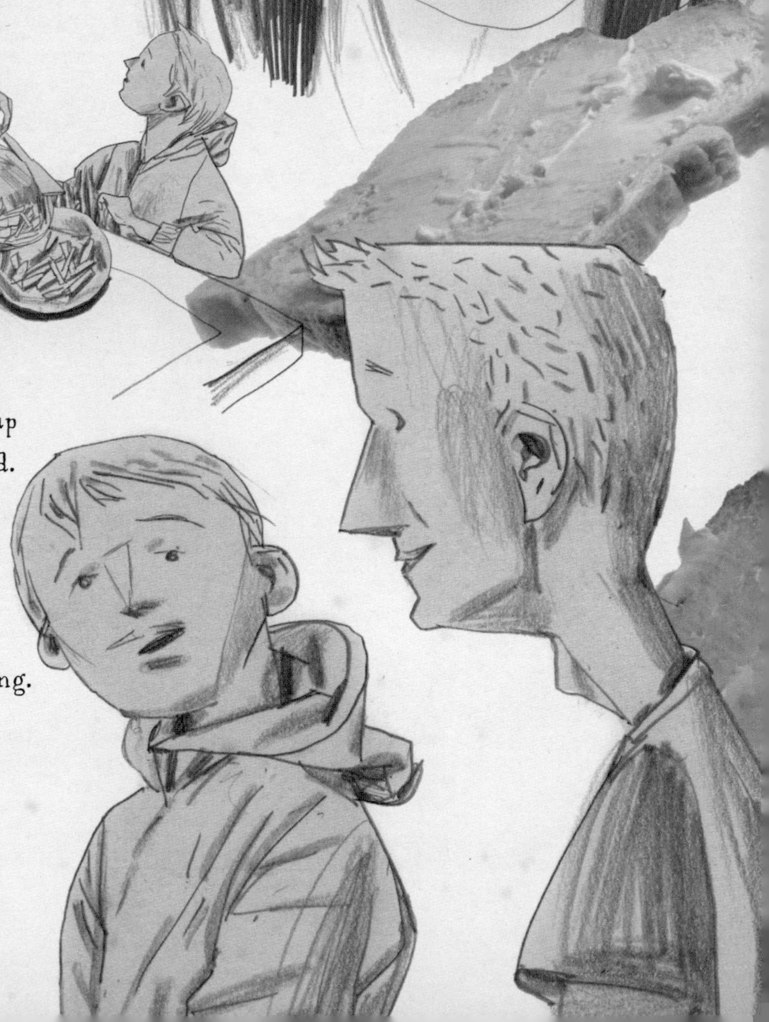

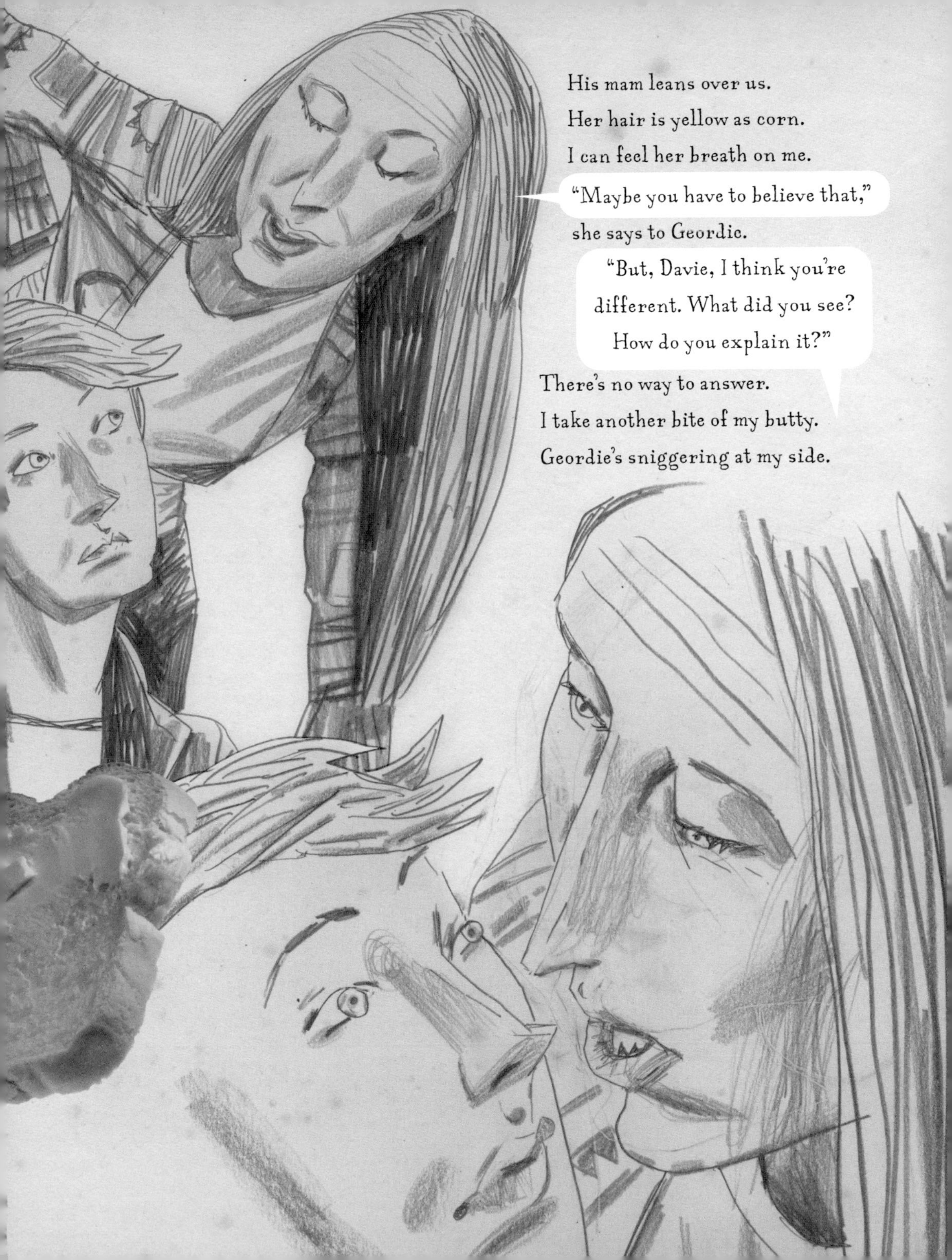
His mam leans over us.
Her hair is yellow as corn.
I can feel her breath on me.
"Maybe you have to believe that,"
she says to Geordie.
"But, Davie, I think you're different. What did you see? How do you explain it?"
There's no way to answer.
I take another bite of my butty.
Geordie's sniggering at my side.

Mrs. Quinn rests her hand on my head.

"Just be quiet for a moment," she says to me.

"Relax and try to feel what is happening in this place. Feel what Joe and I feel, even on a sunny afternoon in an ordinary house on an ordinary estate. There is a disturbance. We are passing through some kind of vortex. Can you feel it, Davie?"

I can feel that Geordie wants to get away but I can't move. Mrs. Quinn moves her hand over my scalp and I go dizzy.

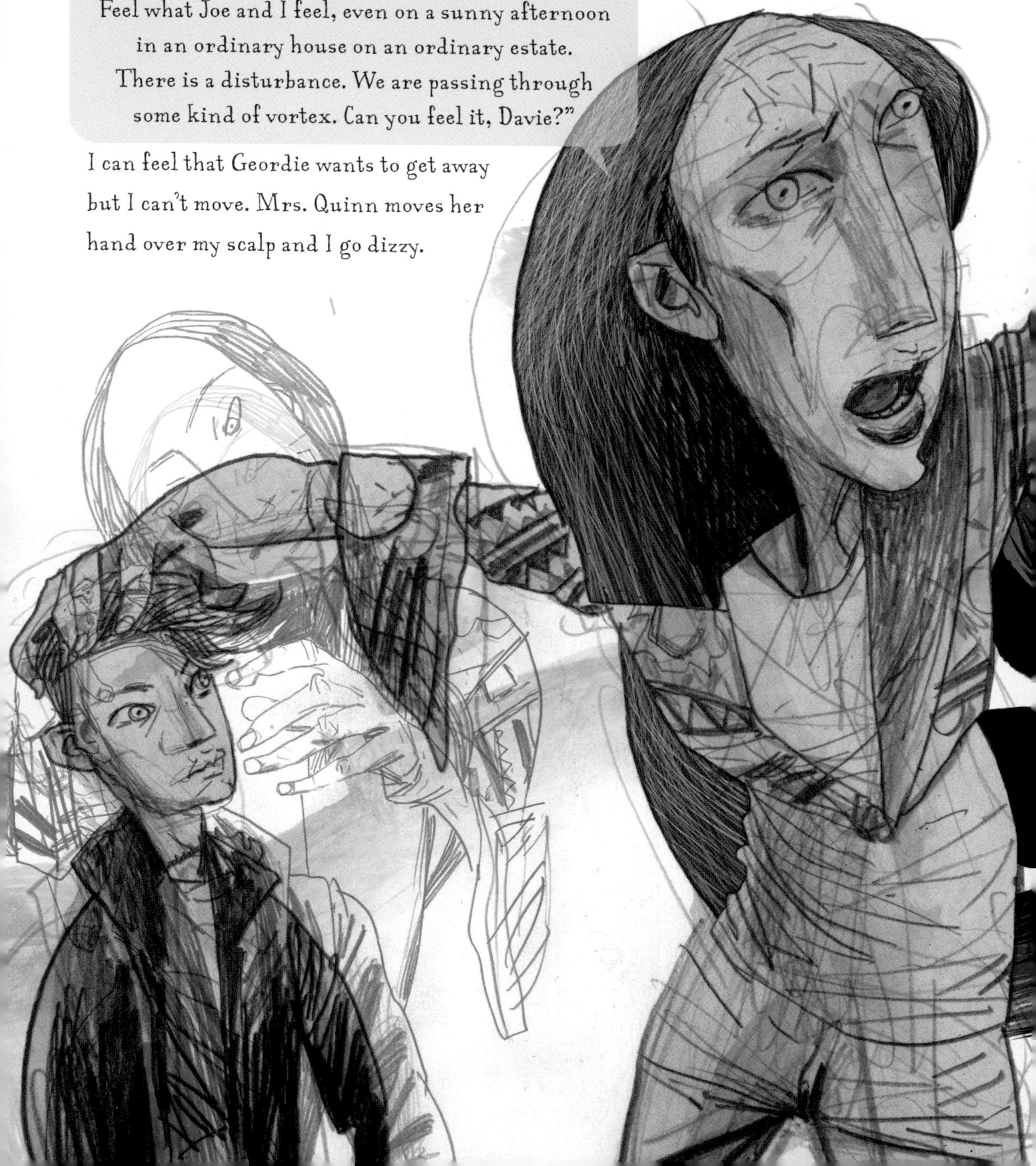

"Just imagine," she murmurs,
"what it is like at night, when the chairs are
shifting and the doors are banging and . . ."
Geordie snorts.
There's a dog howling somewhere.
There's the sound of something
breaking upstairs.

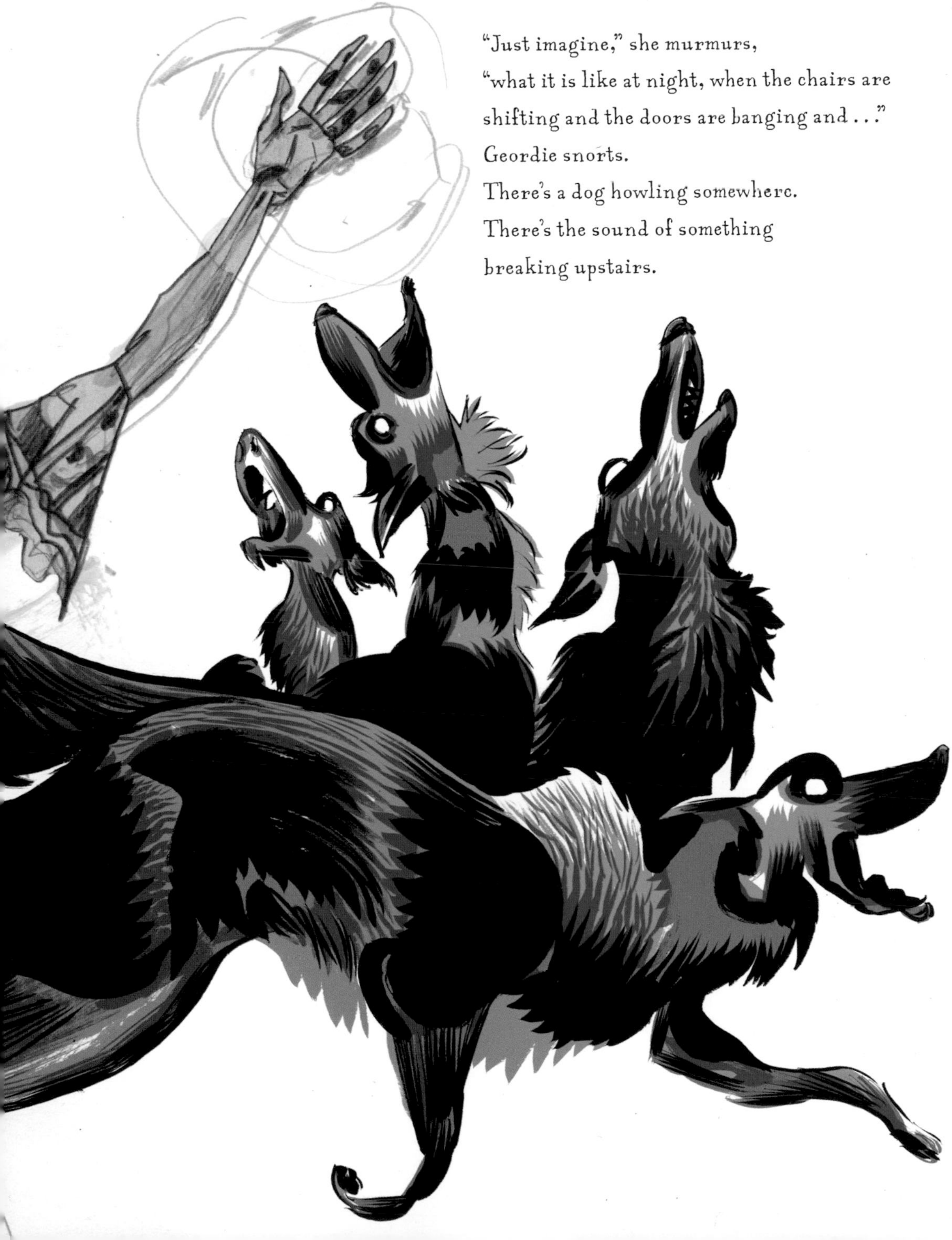

Mrs. Quinn takes her hand away. She stares at the ceiling.
"Did you sense something?" she says softly.
I don't know how to answer.
"You did," she says. "I know it. Only special people can.
We are surrounded by strange forces."
Geordie snorts again. He stuffs some chips into his mouth.
"Howay, Davie," he says. "Time to go."
"You're a churchgoer, aren't you, Davie?" says Mrs. Quinn.
"Yes, I know you are. You understand things like this,
don't you? Things beyond our ken."
"Ken who?" mutters Geordie.
"And you have your priests," Mrs. Quinn goes on.
"Maybe you could talk of this to your priest. Maybe he could come
and rid us of our poltergeist and bring this house some peace.
Maybe he'll feel it's his duty."

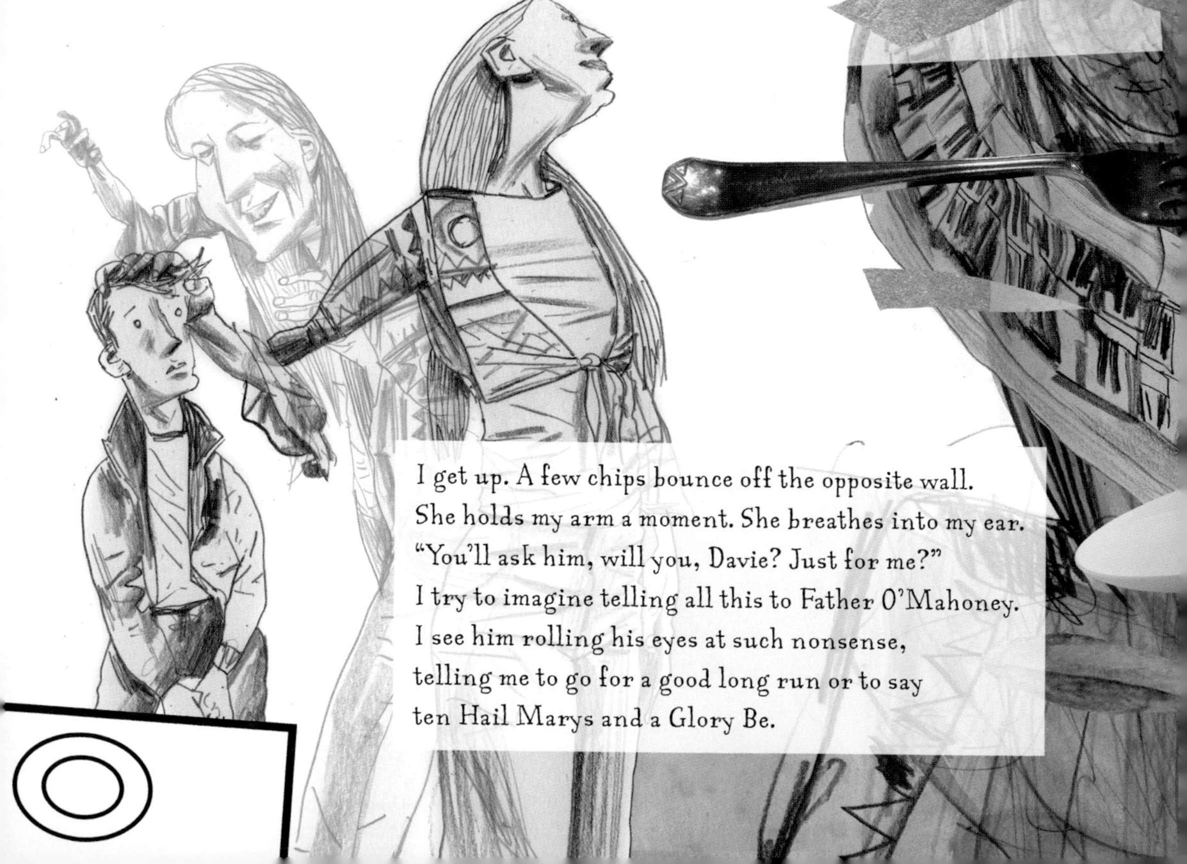

I get up. A few chips bounce off the opposite wall.
She holds my arm a moment. She breathes into my ear.
"You'll ask him, will you, Davie? Just for me?"
I try to imagine telling all this to Father O'Mahoney.
I see him rolling his eyes at such nonsense,
telling me to go for a good long run or to say
ten Hail Marys and a Glory Be.

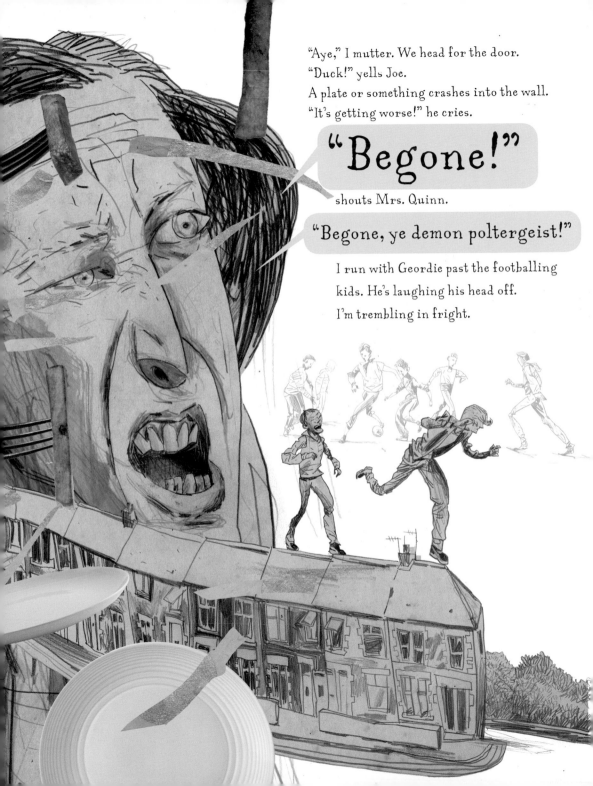

"Aye," I mutter. We head for the door.
"Duck!" yells Joe.
A plate or something crashes into the wall.
"It's getting worse!" he cries.

"Begone!"

shouts Mrs. Quinn.

"Begone, ye demon poltergeist!"

I run with Geordie past the footballing
kids. He's laughing his head off.
I'm trembling in fright.

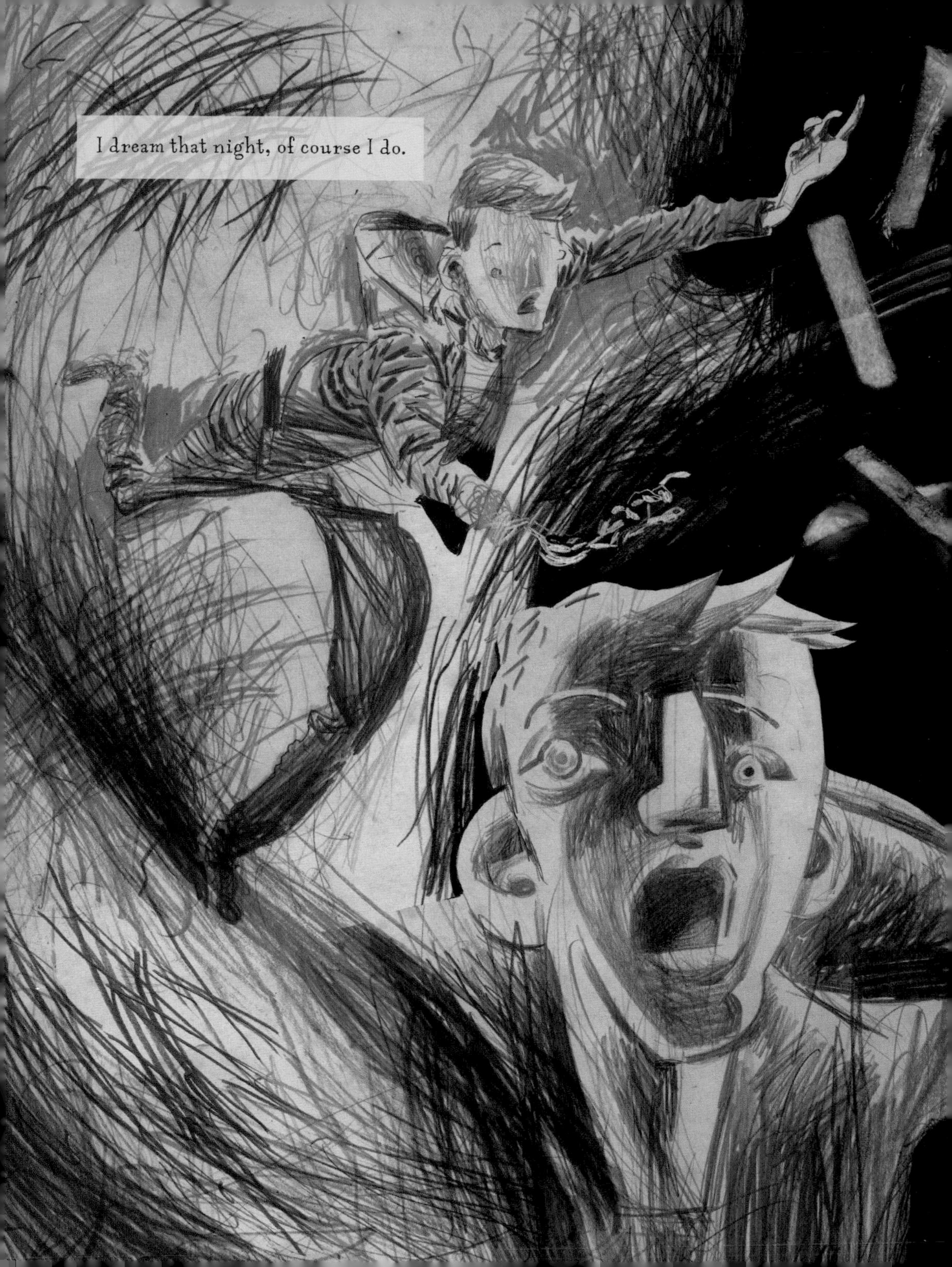
I dream that night, of course I do.

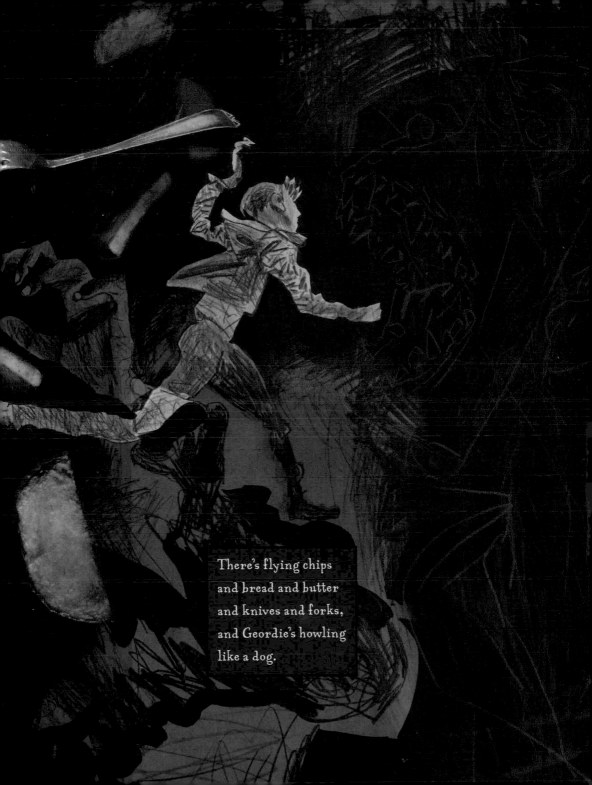

There's flying chips
and bread and butter
and knives and forks,
and Geordie's howling
like a dog.

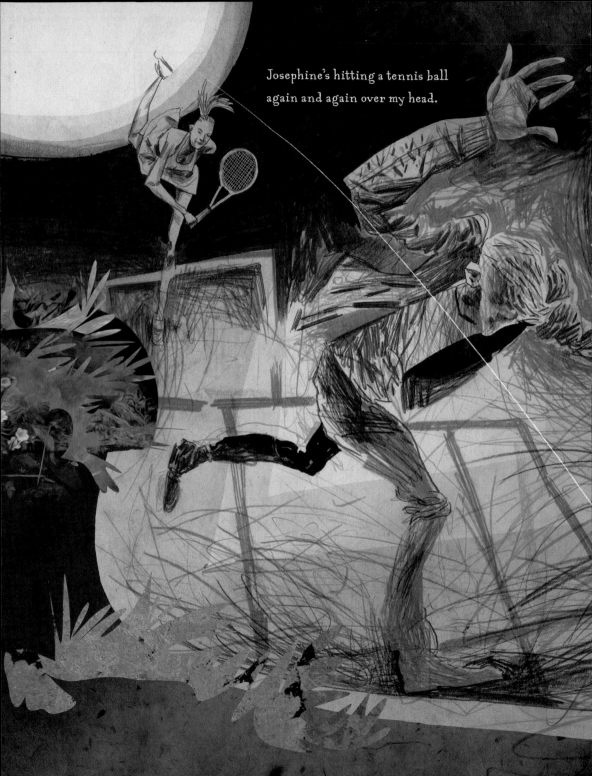

Josephine's hitting a tennis ball
again and again over my head.

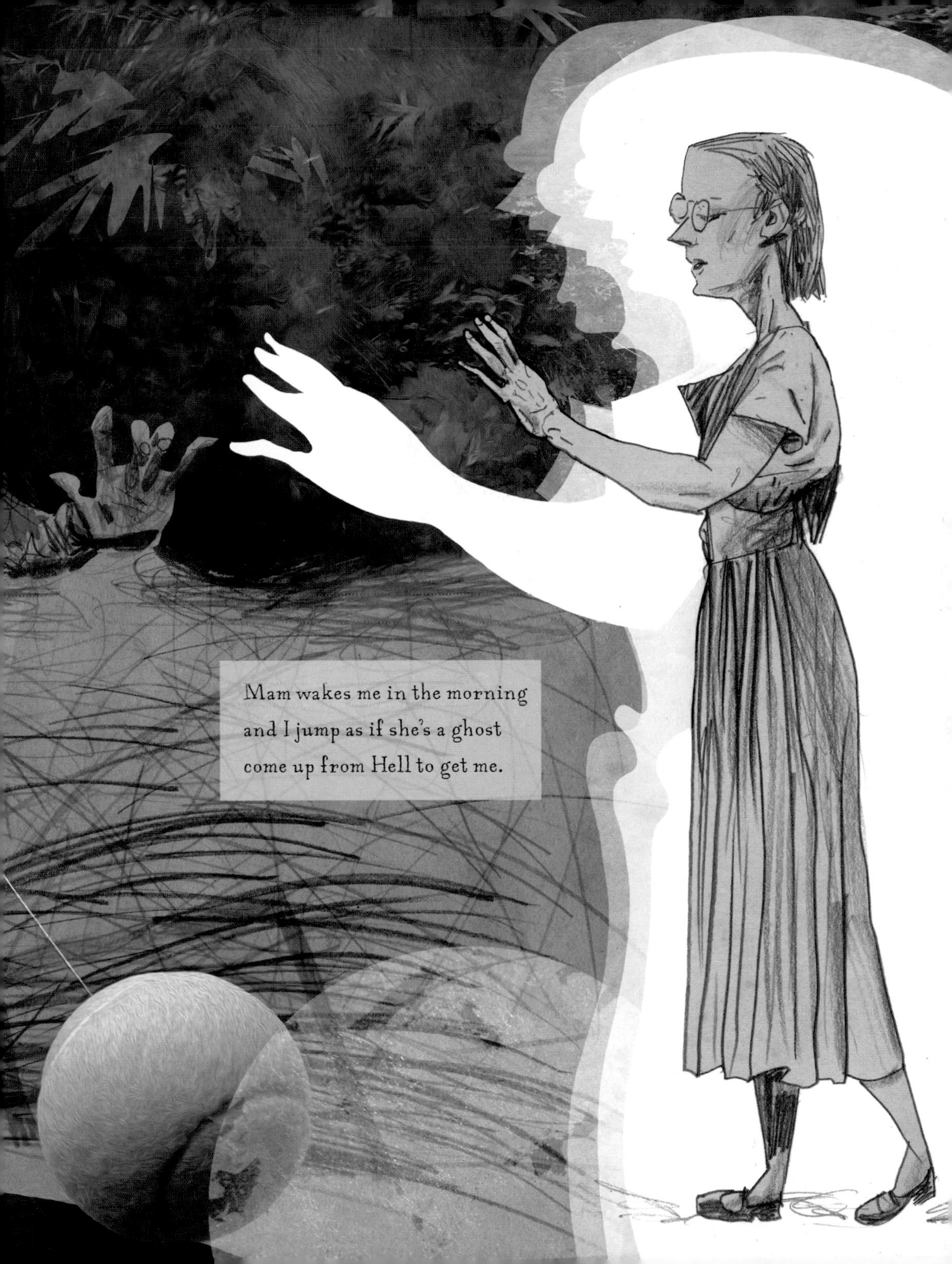
Mam wakes me in the morning and I jump as if she's a ghost come up from Hell to get me.

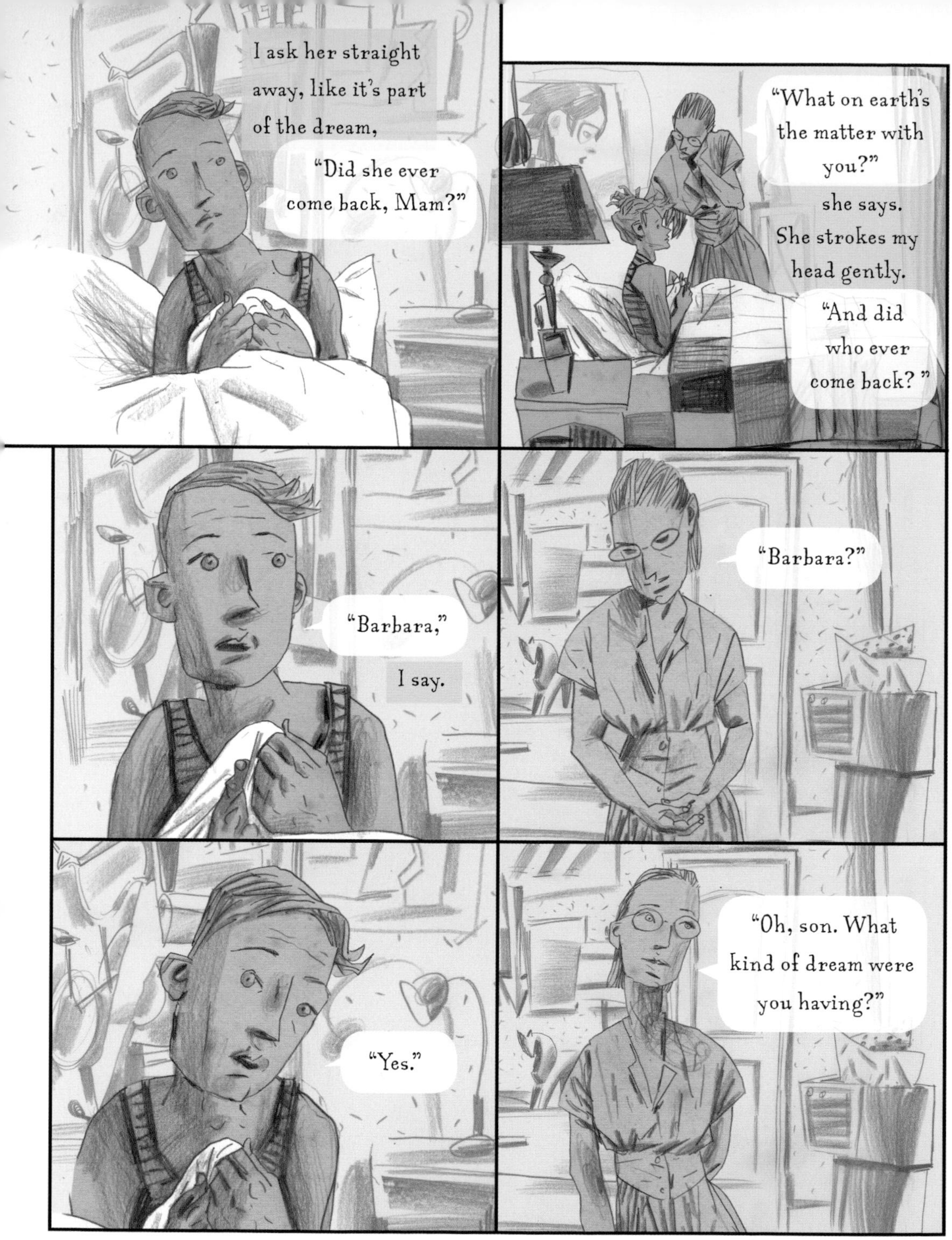
I ask her straight away, like it's part of the dream,
"Did she ever come back, Mam?"
"What on earth's the matter with you?"
she says. She strokes my head gently.
"And did who ever come back?"
"Barbara,"
I say.
"Barbara?"
"Yes."
"Oh, son. What kind of dream were you having?"

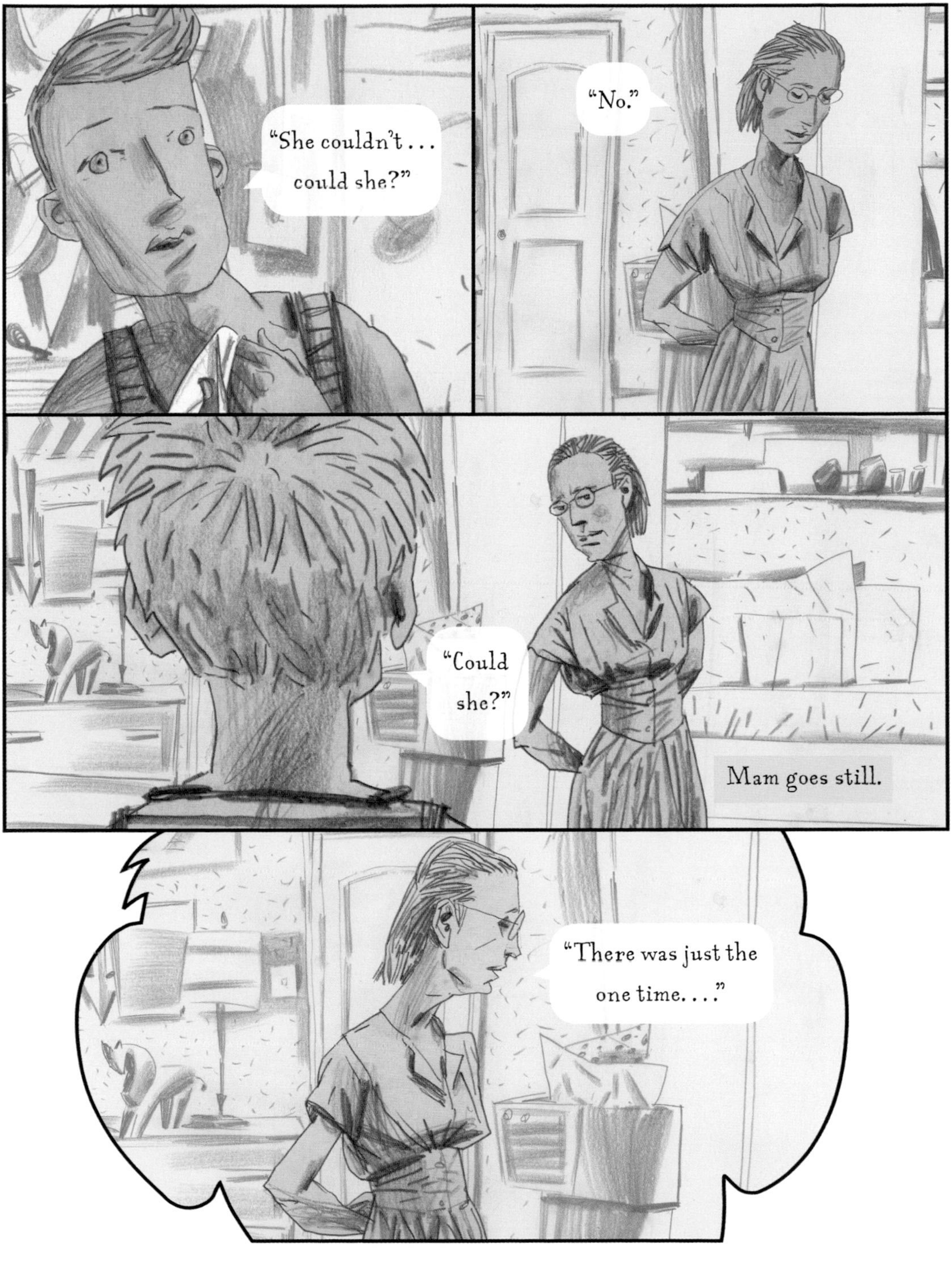
"She couldn't . . . could she?"
"No."
"Could she?"
Mam goes still.
"There was just the one time. . . ."

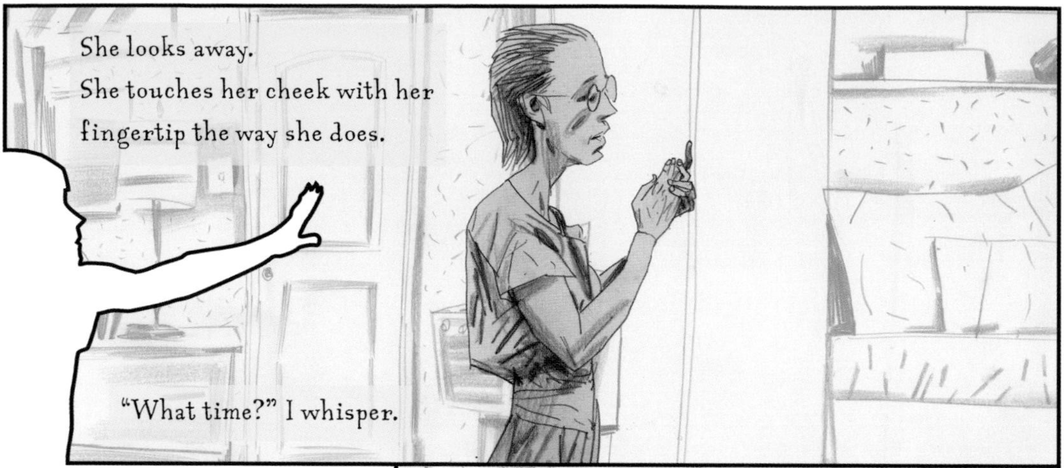
She looks away.
She touches her cheek with her
fingertip the way she does.
"What time?" I whisper.

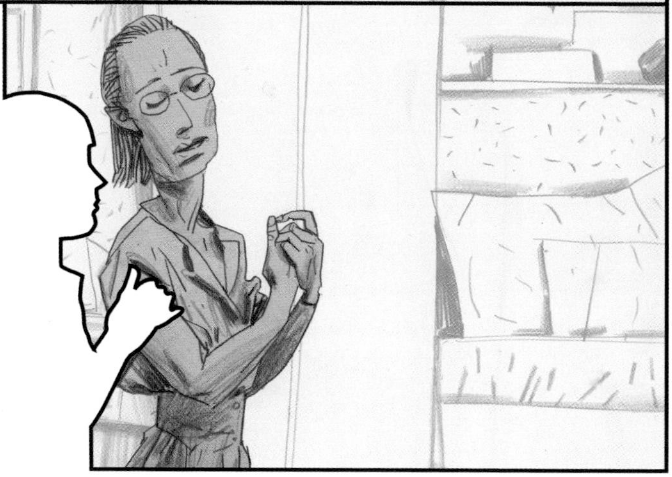

"I felt her touch me, son,
on my shoulder.
A couple of weeks after . . ."

I wait. I watch.

"I heard her whispering,
'I'm all right, Mammy.
Don't worry, Mammy,
I'm all right.'"

"Did you see her?"

"No. And it was just the once.
Maybe it was just a . . .
But it felt like her, son.
It made me feel . . .
I didn't feel so desolate."
She sighs.

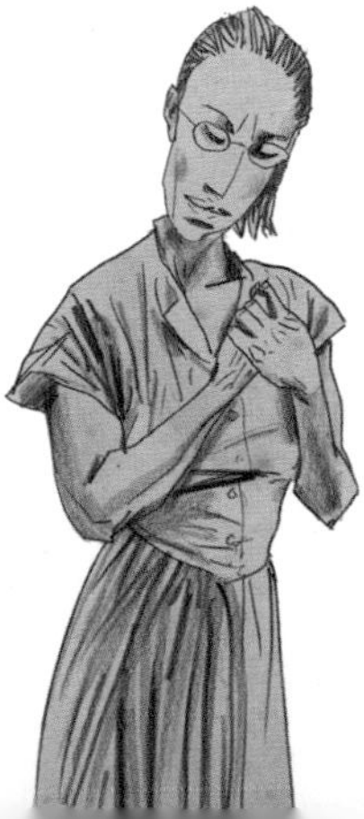

"I didn't tell you.
I didn't want to upset you."
Then her eyes are shining
as she smiles.

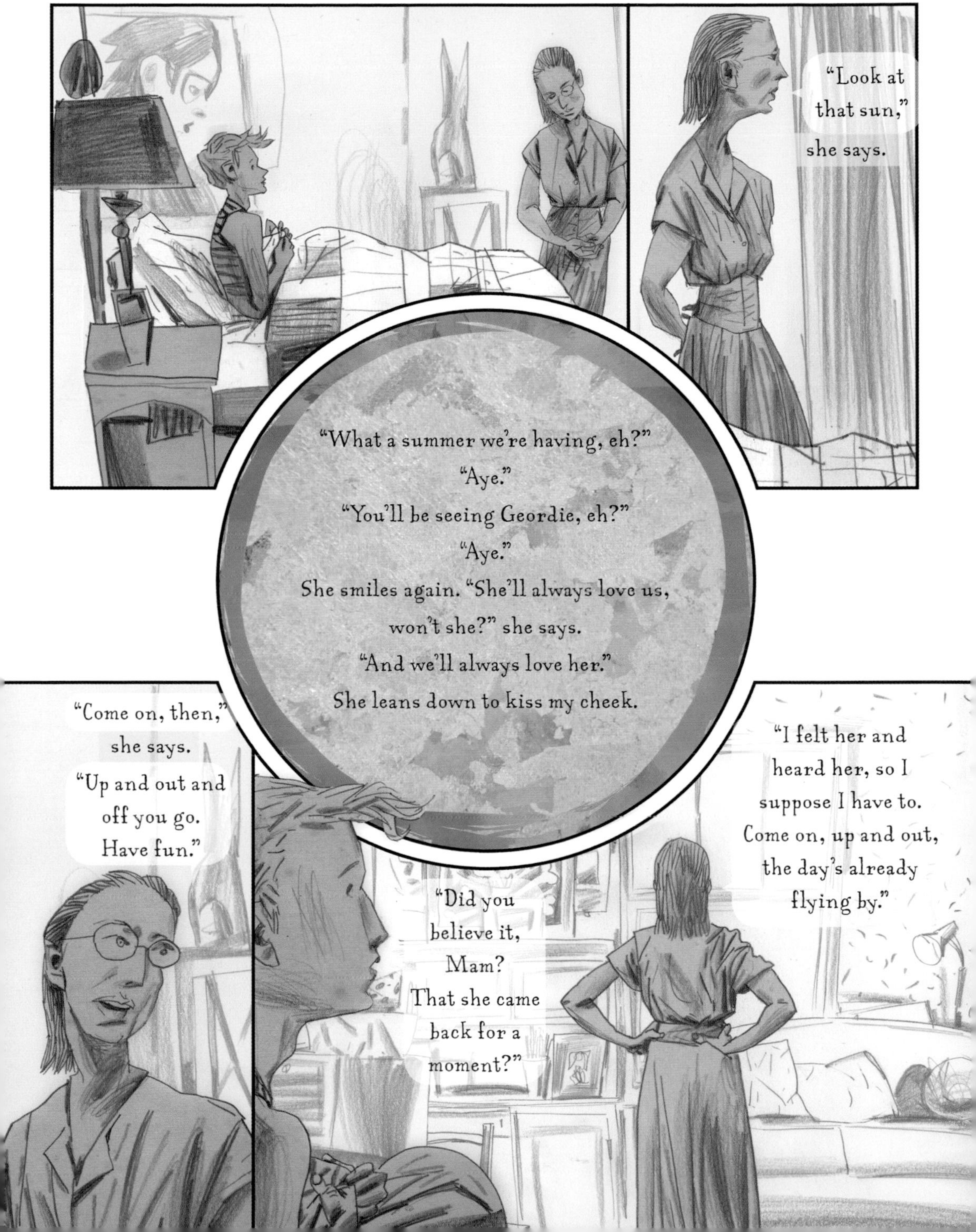
"Look at that sun,"
she says.
"What a summer we're having, eh?"
"Aye."
"You'll be seeing Geordie, eh?"
"Aye."
She smiles again. "She'll always love us, won't she?" she says.
"And we'll always love her."
She leans down to kiss my cheek.
"Come on, then,"
she says.
"Up and out and off you go. Have fun."
"Did you believe it, Mam? That she came back for a moment?"
"I felt her and heard her, so I suppose I have to. Come on, up and out, the day's already flying by."

I head for Geordie's but I keep scanning the streets for Josephine. I pass by the park and listen for the pop and thump of racquets and balls. When I turn the corner by the Co-op, I bump right into Father Kelly in his long black gown. He's the new young priest, straight from Ireland.

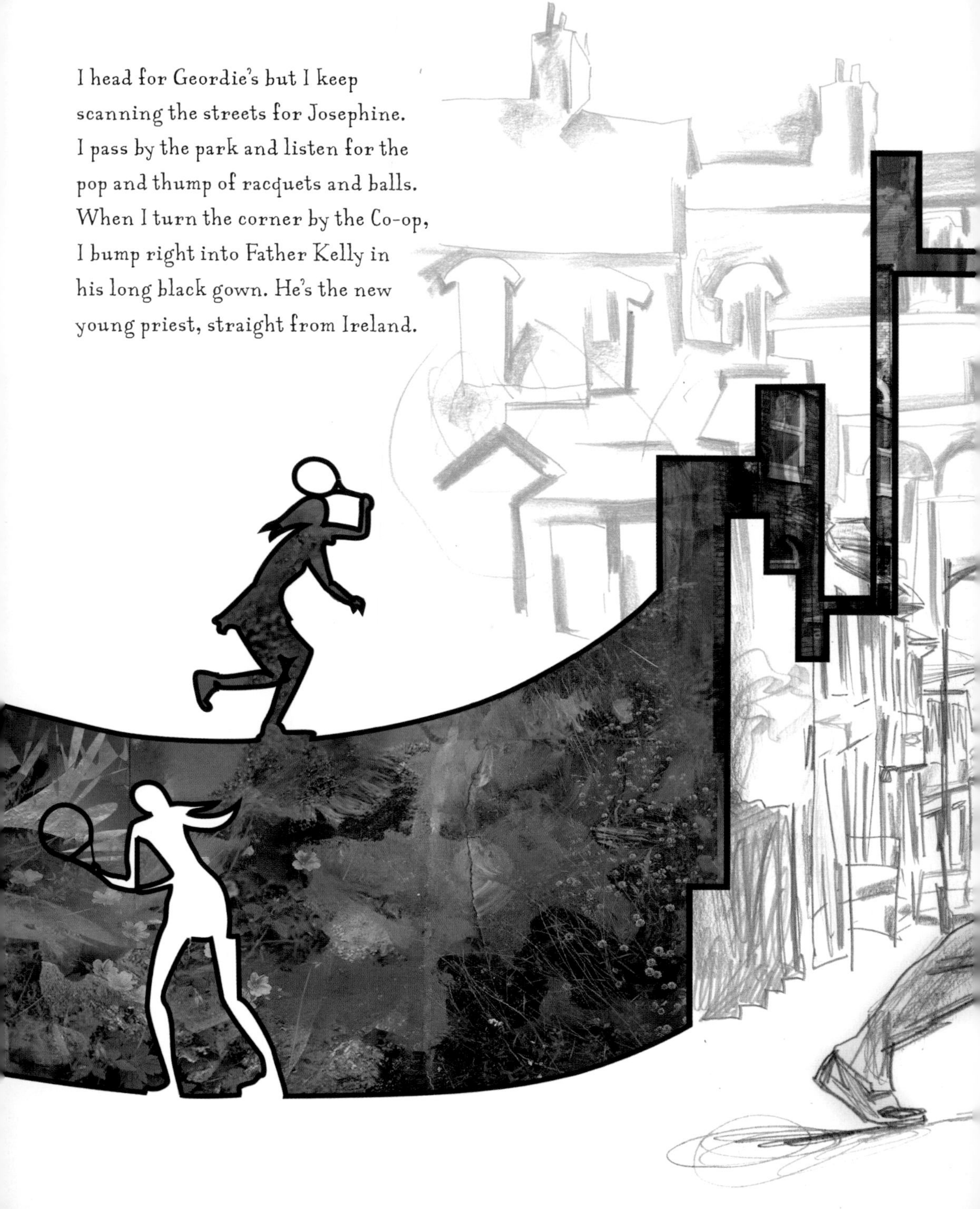

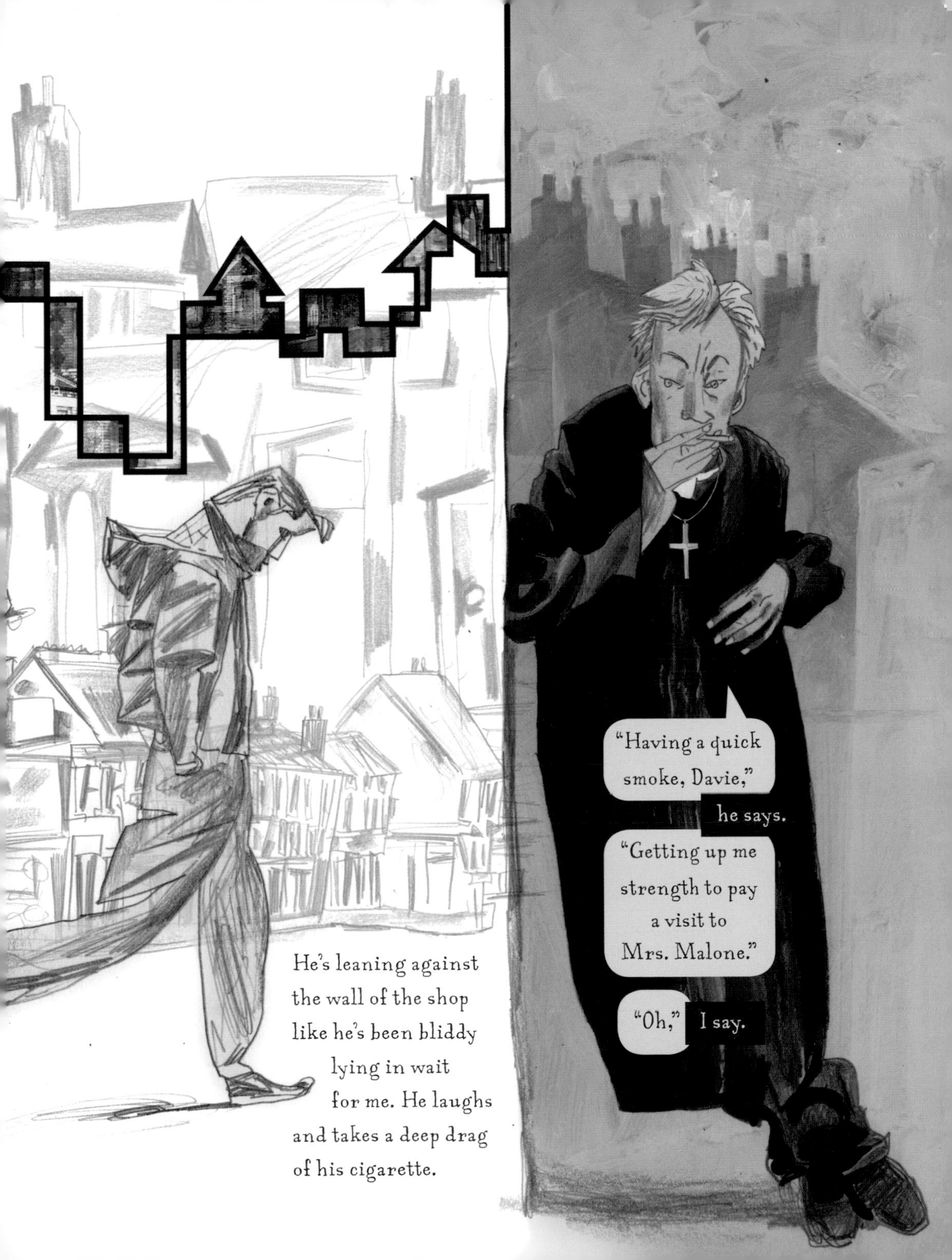
He's leaning against the wall of the shop like he's been bliddy lying in wait for me. He laughs and takes a deep drag of his cigarette.
"Having a quick smoke, Davie,"
he says.
"Getting up me strength to pay a visit to Mrs. Malone."
"Oh,"
I say.

"She'd test the faith of
St. bliddy Francis himself,"
he says. He makes a quick
sign of the cross.
"'Scuse the French.
Off to Geordie's, are you?"

"Yes, Father."

"Good lad. Make the most of it."
He holds out his cigarette.
"Want a drag or two?"
I don't move. He laughs again.
"I know some of you
boys get started early."

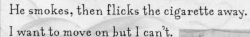

He smokes, then flicks the cigarette away.
I want to move on but I can't.
It seems like he's the same.
"You know her?" he says.
"The Missus Malone?"
"A bit, Father."
"They say she's lapsed," he tells me.
"They say other things."
He lights another cigarette.
"You've heard?" he asks.
"Dunno, Father."
"Best not to. These things
are sent to test us."

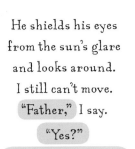

He shields his eyes
from the sun's glare
and looks around.
I still can't move.
"Father," I say.
"Yes?"
"I think I'm starting
to believe in things I
shouldn't."

"Protestantism?" he says.
"No, Father."
"Atheism?"
"No, Father."
I hear kids laughing in the park.

"It's never Sunderland!"
he exclaims.
"No, Father."

"Well, that all
seems pretty safe.
Your seat in
Heaven is assured."

He moves his hand
through the air in blessing.

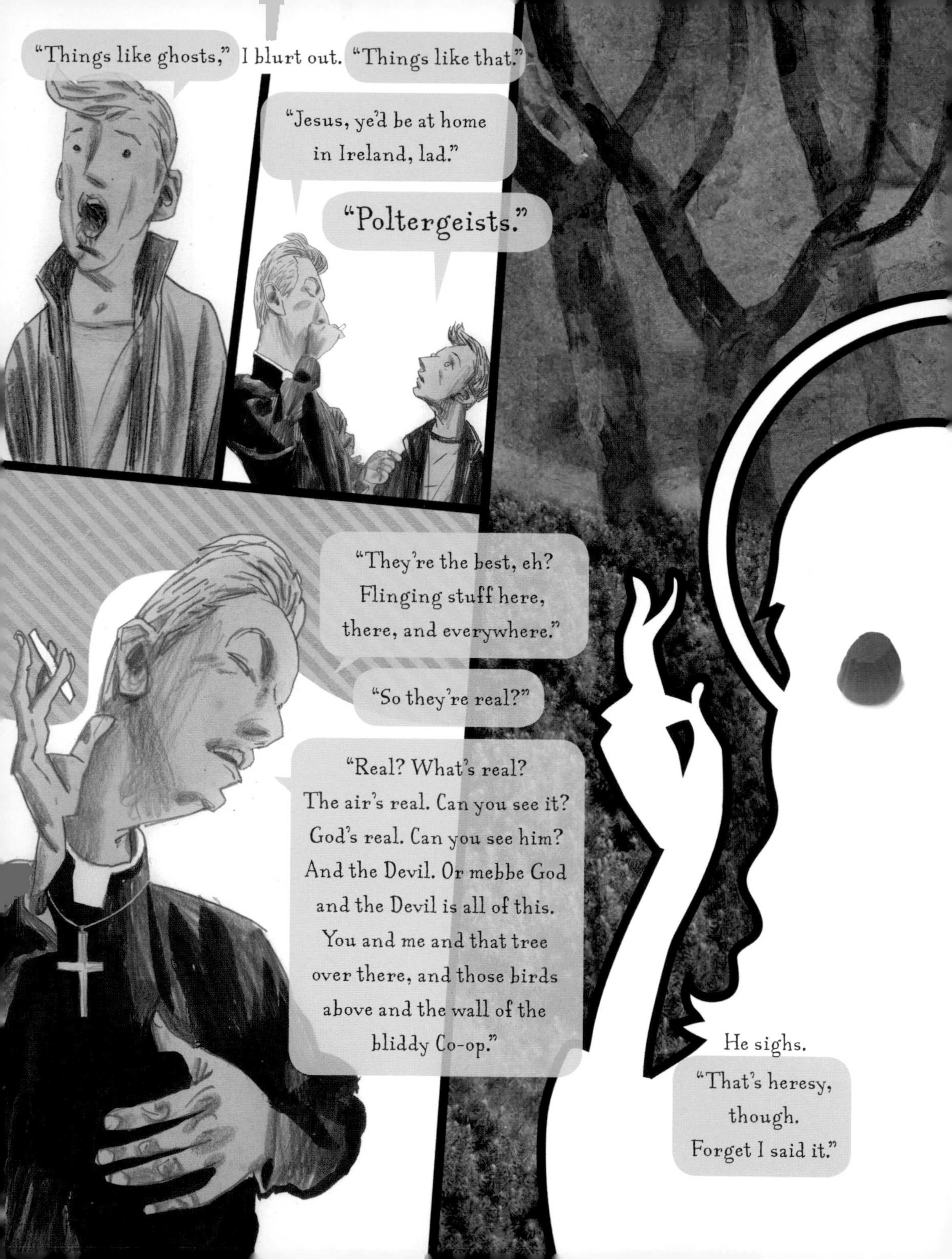

"Things like ghosts," I blurt out. "Things like that."
"Jesus, ye'd be at home in Ireland, lad."
"Poltergeists."
"They're the best, eh? Flinging stuff here, there, and everywhere."
"So they're real?"
"Real? What's real? The air's real. Can you see it? God's real. Can you see him? And the Devil. Or mebbe God and the Devil is all of this. You and me and that tree over there, and those birds above and the wall of the bliddy Co-op."
He sighs.
"That's heresy, though. Forget I said it."

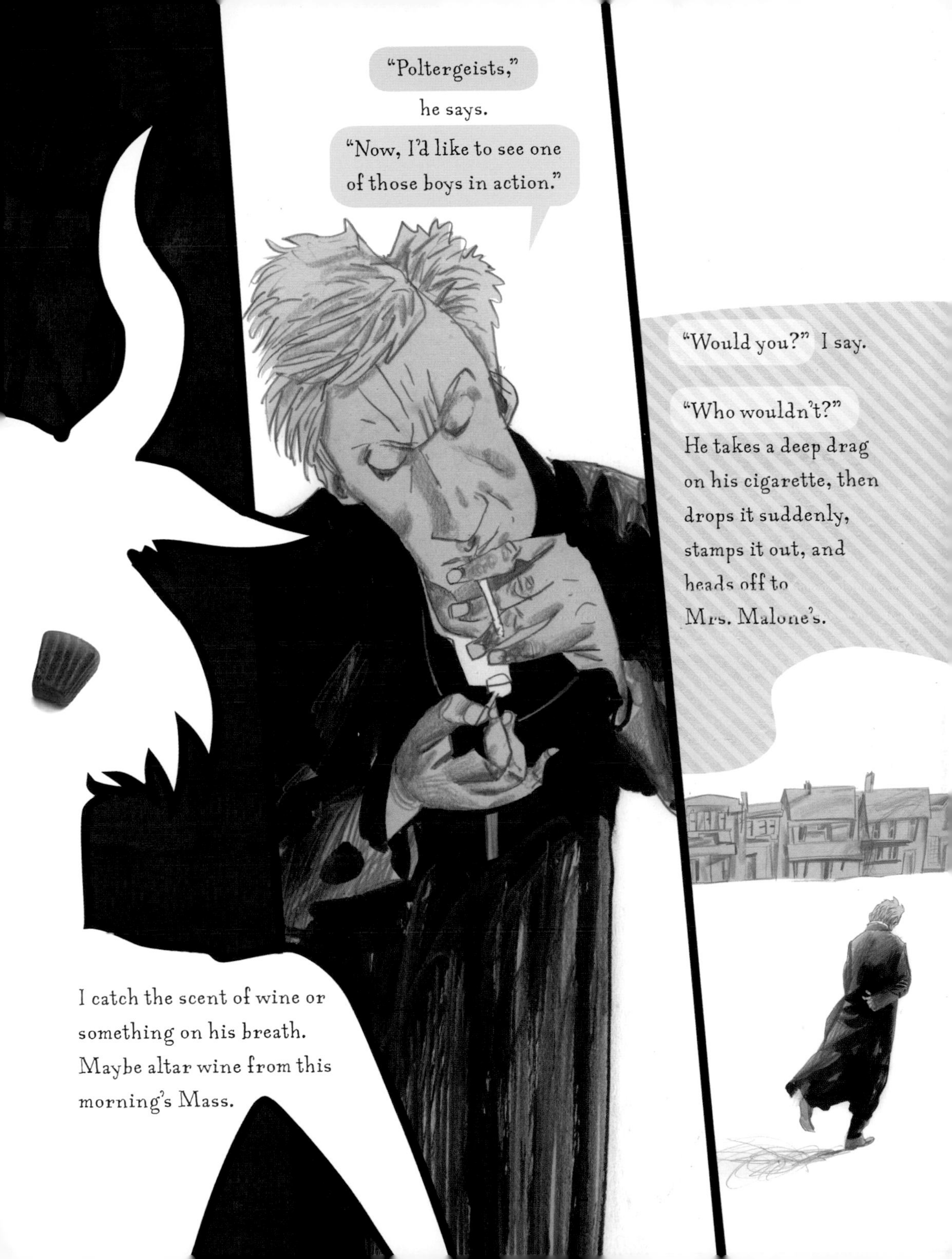
"Poltergeists,"
he says.
"Now, I'd like to see one of those boys in action."
I catch the scent of wine or something on his breath. Maybe altar wine from this morning's Mass.
"Would you?" I say.
"Who wouldn't?"
He takes a deep drag on his cigarette, then drops it suddenly, stamps it out, and heads off to Mrs. Malone's.

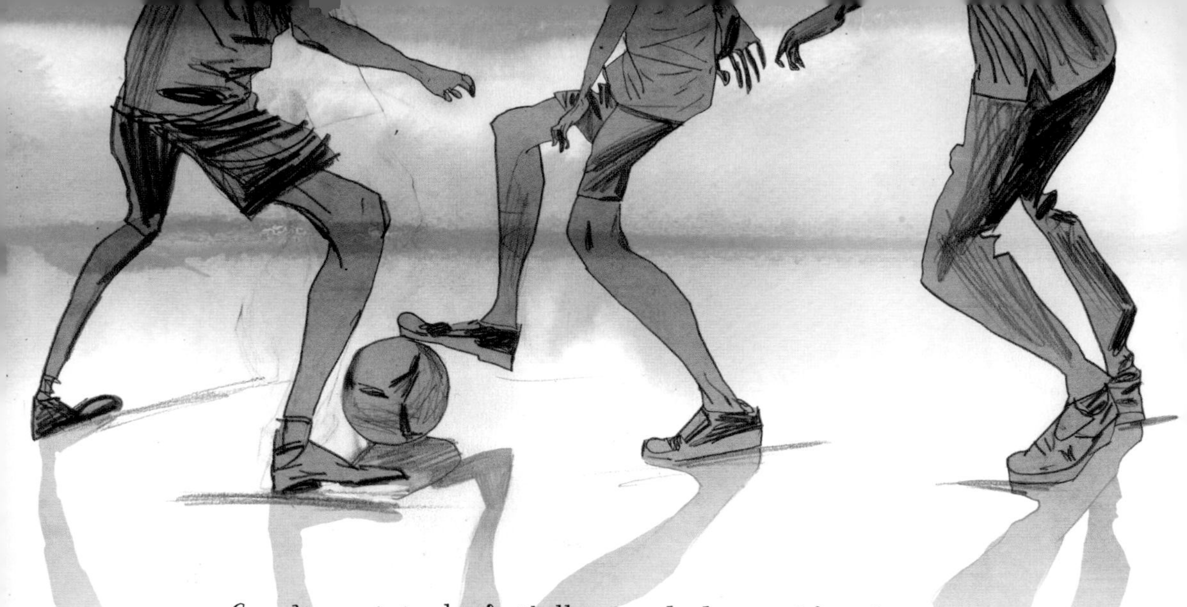

Geordie wants to play football and we kick around for a bit in his front street, but I'm hopeless. I can't help it. I'm drawn back to Joe's. Can't think about anything else. I tell him I think we should go again.

"Did you not see?" Geordie says. "It was Joe chucking all the stuff around. It's just Joe bliddy Quinn being Joe bliddy Quinn. And she's letting him."

"There was something," I say.

"So now you're sticking up for him when you're the one who always says he's just a freak."

"I'm not sticking up for him! It's nothing to do with him. It's —"

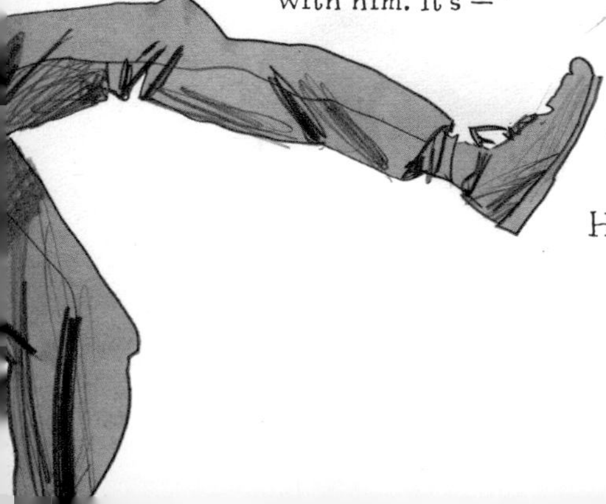

He snorts. "Oh, I impugn you!" he mocks. "I am so sorry. We are surrounded by strange forces!"

He chips the ball into the air, knees it, heads it, then lashes it into the front garden wall.

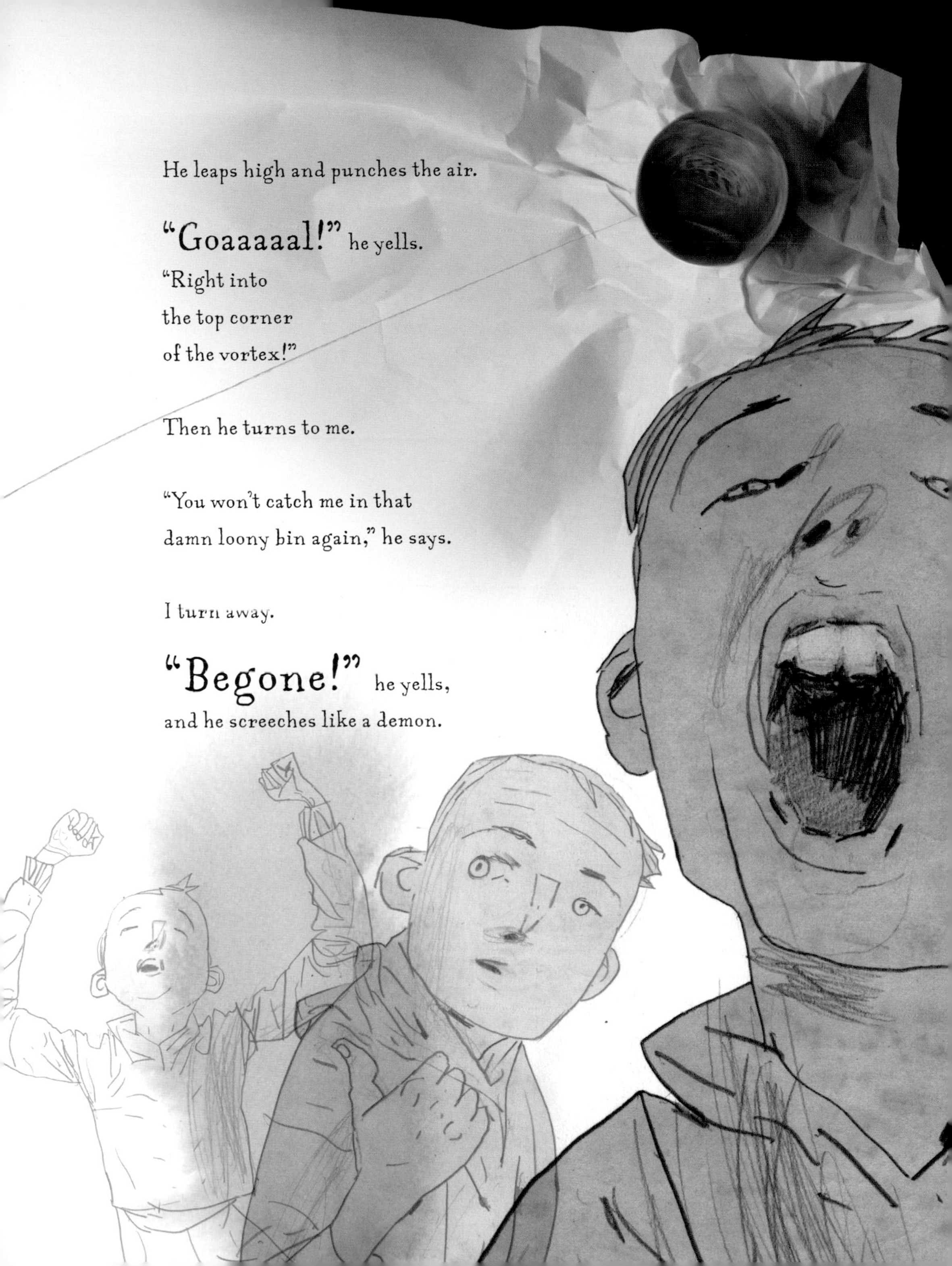

He leaps high and punches the air.

"Goaaaaal!" he yells.
"Right into
the top corner
of the vortex!"

Then he turns to me.

"You won't catch me in that
damn loony bin again," he says.

I turn away.

"Begone!" he yells,
and he screeches like a demon.

I go up onto the top fields and lie there, and the long grass waves above my eyes. The sun's bright, the sky's blue, the larks are singing wild. Sometimes a thin cloud drifts by. I sit up and look down at everything: the town, its square, its streets, its new estates, its steeples and parks.

Hear the drone of traffic and engines.
The dinning of caulkers in the shipyards on the river far below. Kids squealing somewhere.
I'm sure I can hear the pop of tennis balls.

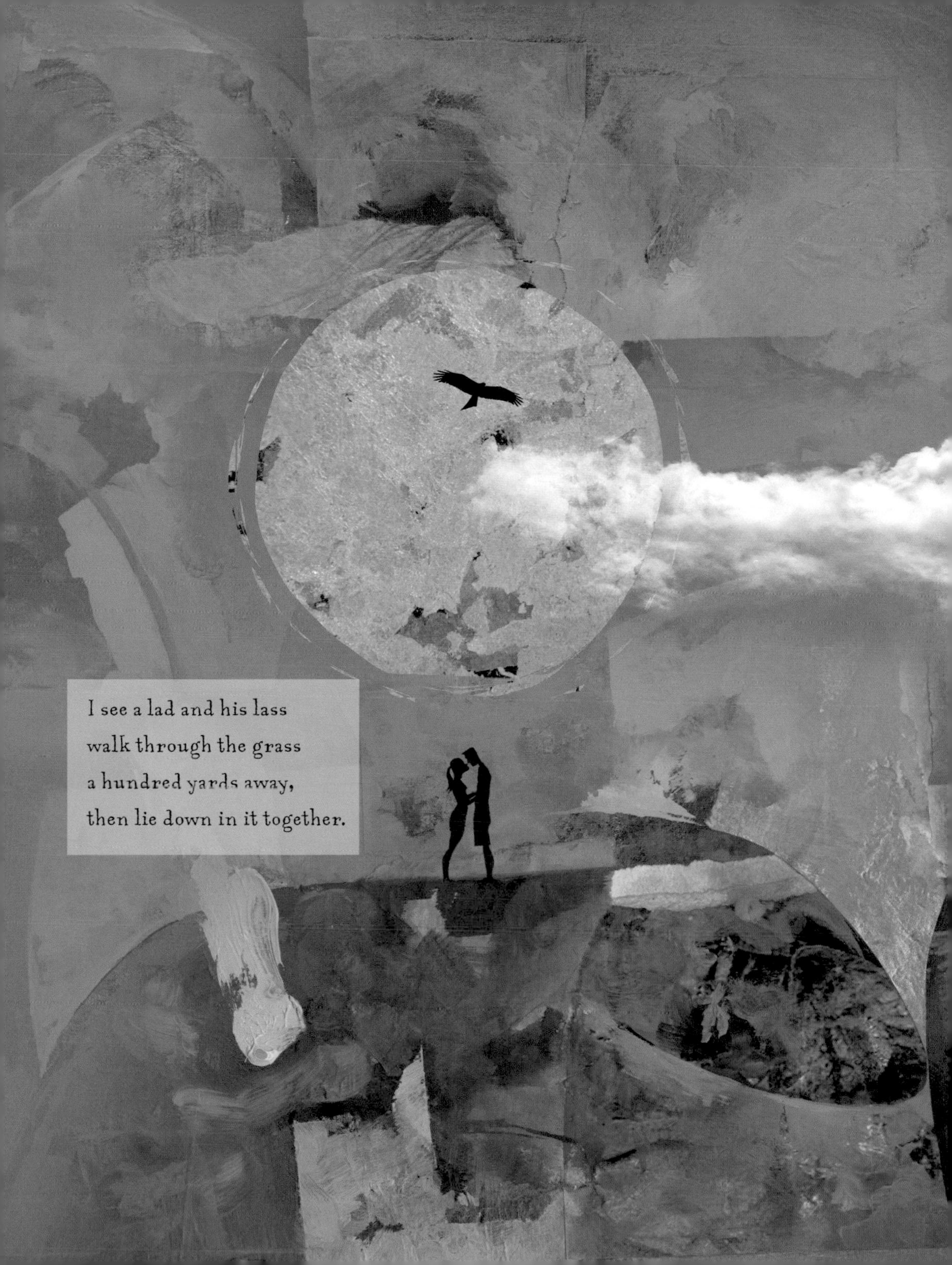

I see a lad and his lass
walk through the grass
a hundred yards away,
then lie down in it together.

The heat comes from the earth and from
the sky. The distant sea's dark blue.
Is this everything, all this stuff around me?
Is this where everything happens?
I think of Barbara, the way she used
to giggle and wave as I arrived
home from school.

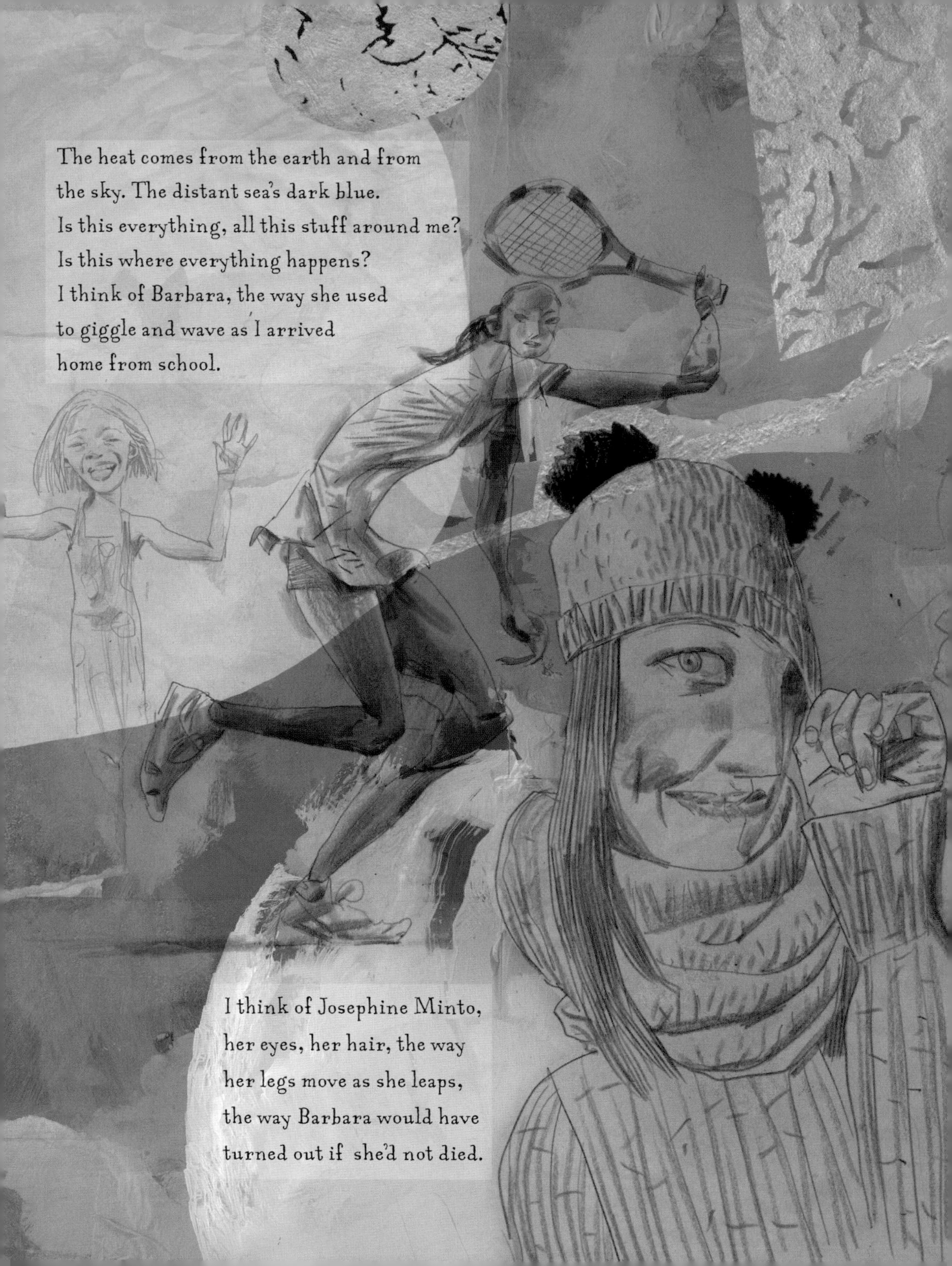

I think of Josephine Minto,
her eyes, her hair, the way
her legs move as she leaps,
the way Barbara would have
turned out if she'd not died.

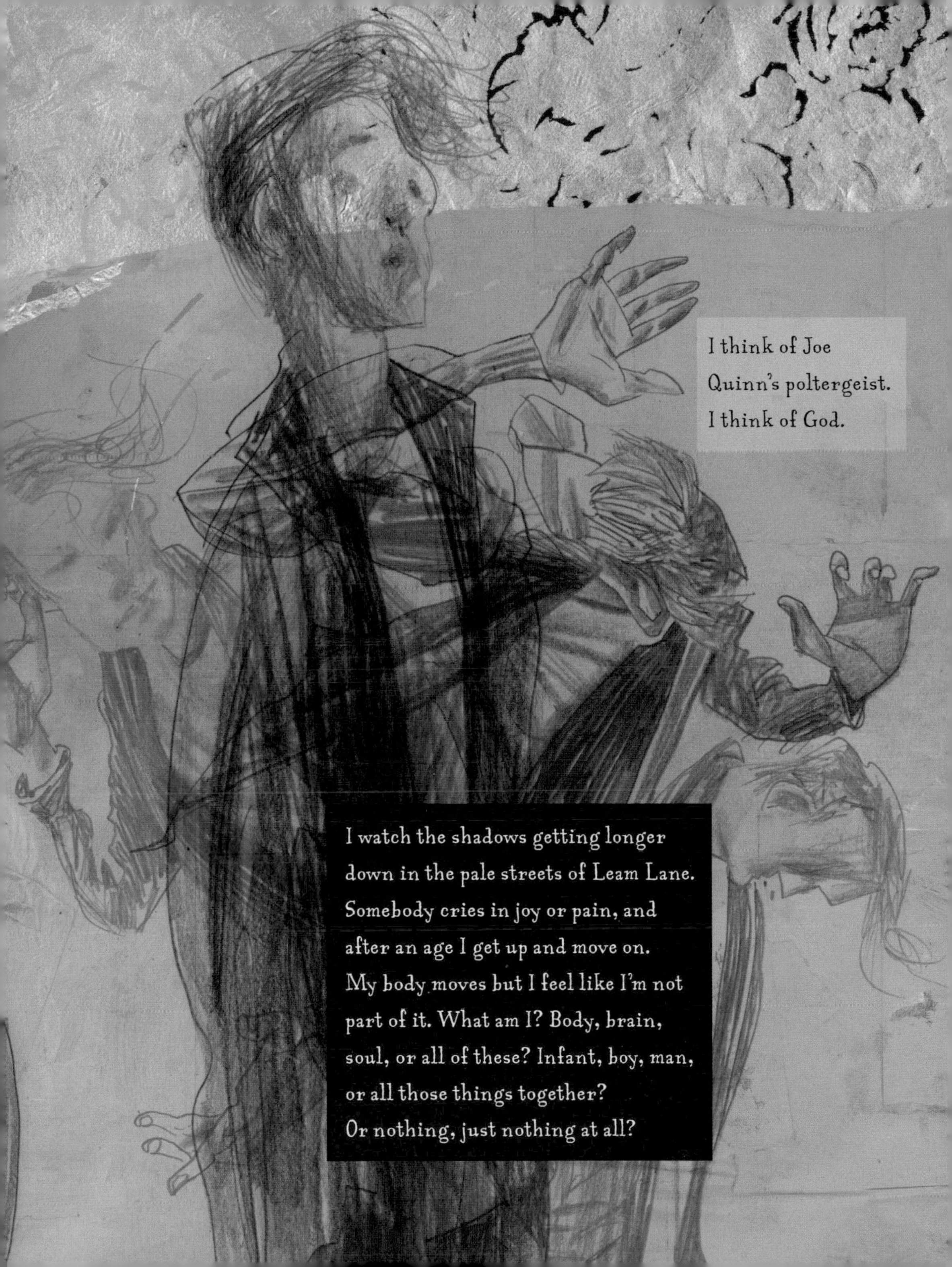
I think of Joe Quinn's poltergeist. I think of God.
I watch the shadows getting longer down in the pale streets of Leam Lane. Somebody cries in joy or pain, and after an age I get up and move on. My body moves but I feel like I'm not part of it. What am I? Body, brain, soul, or all of these? Infant, boy, man, or all those things together? Or nothing, just nothing at all?

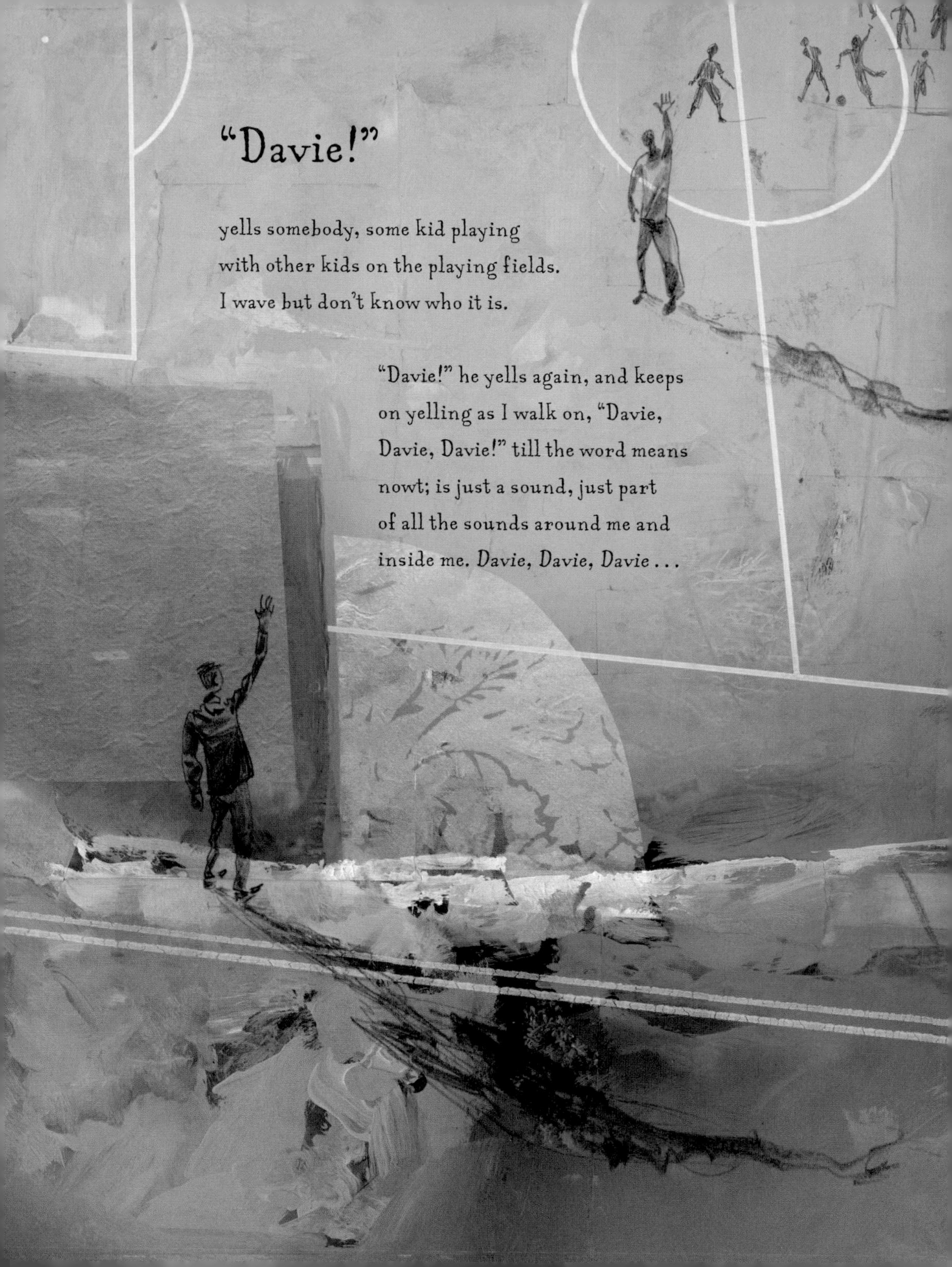

"Davie!"

yells somebody, some kid playing
with other kids on the playing fields.
I wave but don't know who it is.

"Davie!" he yells again, and keeps
on yelling as I walk on, "Davie,
Davie, Davie!" till the word means
nowt; is just a sound, just part
of all the sounds around me and
inside me. *Davie, Davie, Davie . . .*

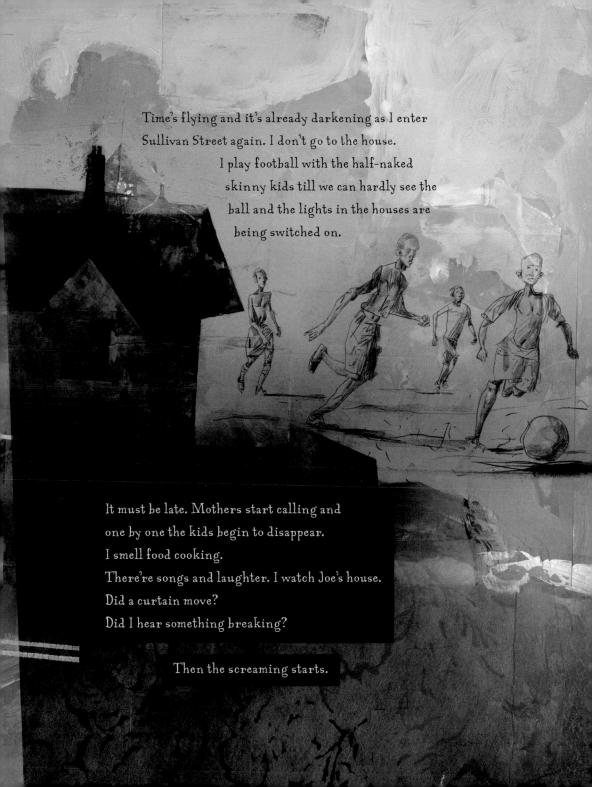

Time's flying and it's already darkening as I enter
Sullivan Street again. I don't go to the house.
        I play football with the half-naked
            skinny kids till we can hardly see the
            ball and the lights in the houses are
            being switched on.

It must be late. Mothers start calling and
one by one the kids begin to disappear.
I smell food cooking.
There're songs and laughter. I watch Joe's house.
Did a curtain move?
Did I hear something breaking?

        Then the screaming starts.

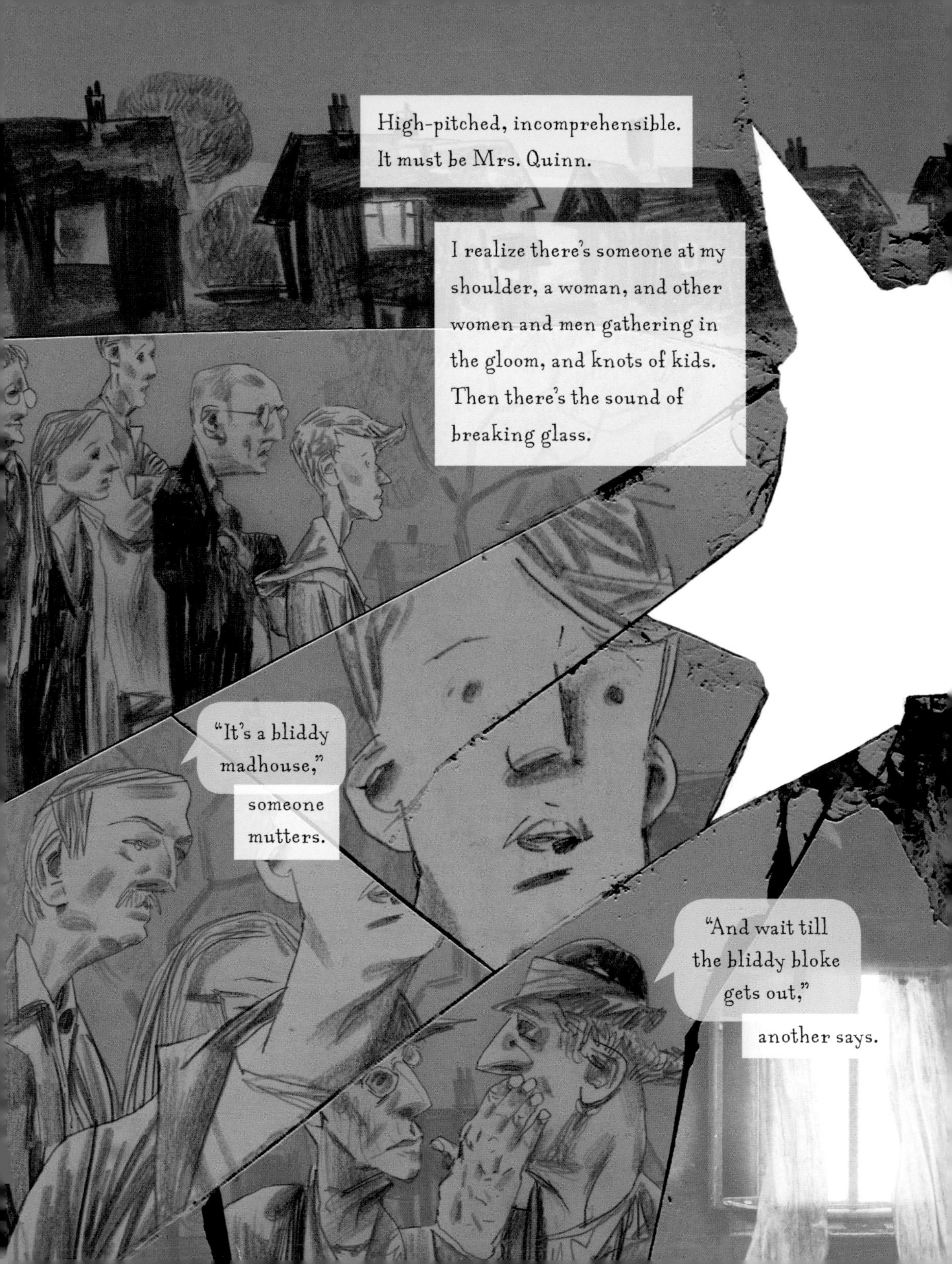
High-pitched, incomprehensible. It must be Mrs. Quinn.
I realize there's someone at my shoulder, a woman, and other women and men gathering in the gloom, and knots of kids. Then there's the sound of breaking glass.
"It's a bliddy madhouse,"
someone mutters.
"And wait till the bliddy bloke gets out,"
another says.

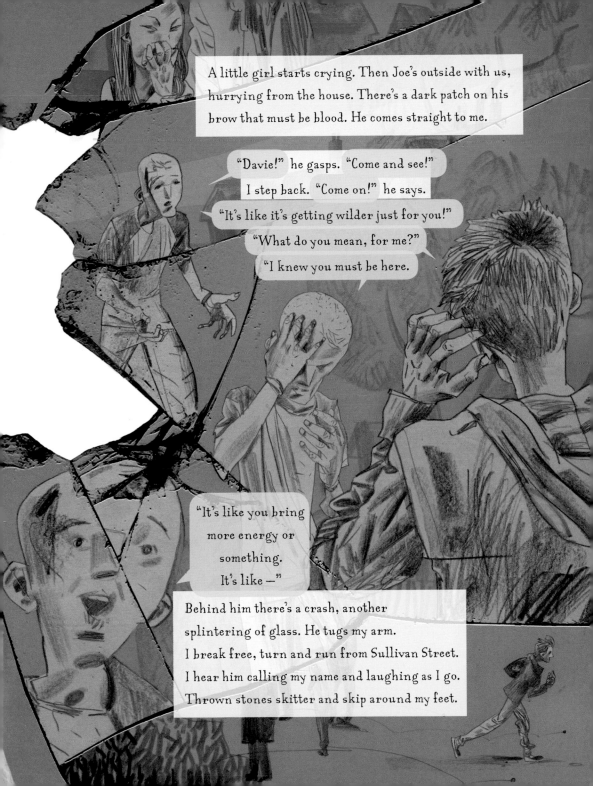

A little girl starts crying. Then Joe's outside with us,
hurrying from the house. There's a dark patch on his
brow that must be blood. He comes straight to me.

"Davie!" he gasps. "Come and see!"
I step back. "Come on!" he says.
"It's like it's getting wilder just for you!"
"What do you mean, for me?"
"I knew you must be here.

"It's like you bring
more energy or
something.
It's like —"

Behind him there's a crash, another
splintering of glass. He tugs my arm.
I break free, turn and run from Sullivan Street.
I hear him calling my name and laughing as I go.
Thrown stones skitter and skip around my feet.

I meet Father Kelly in the street again, two days later.
This time he's stepping out of the Columba Club,
and this time there's beer on his breath.
He's still in his black robes in this August heat.
A wooden crucifix dangles from his throat. He laughs.

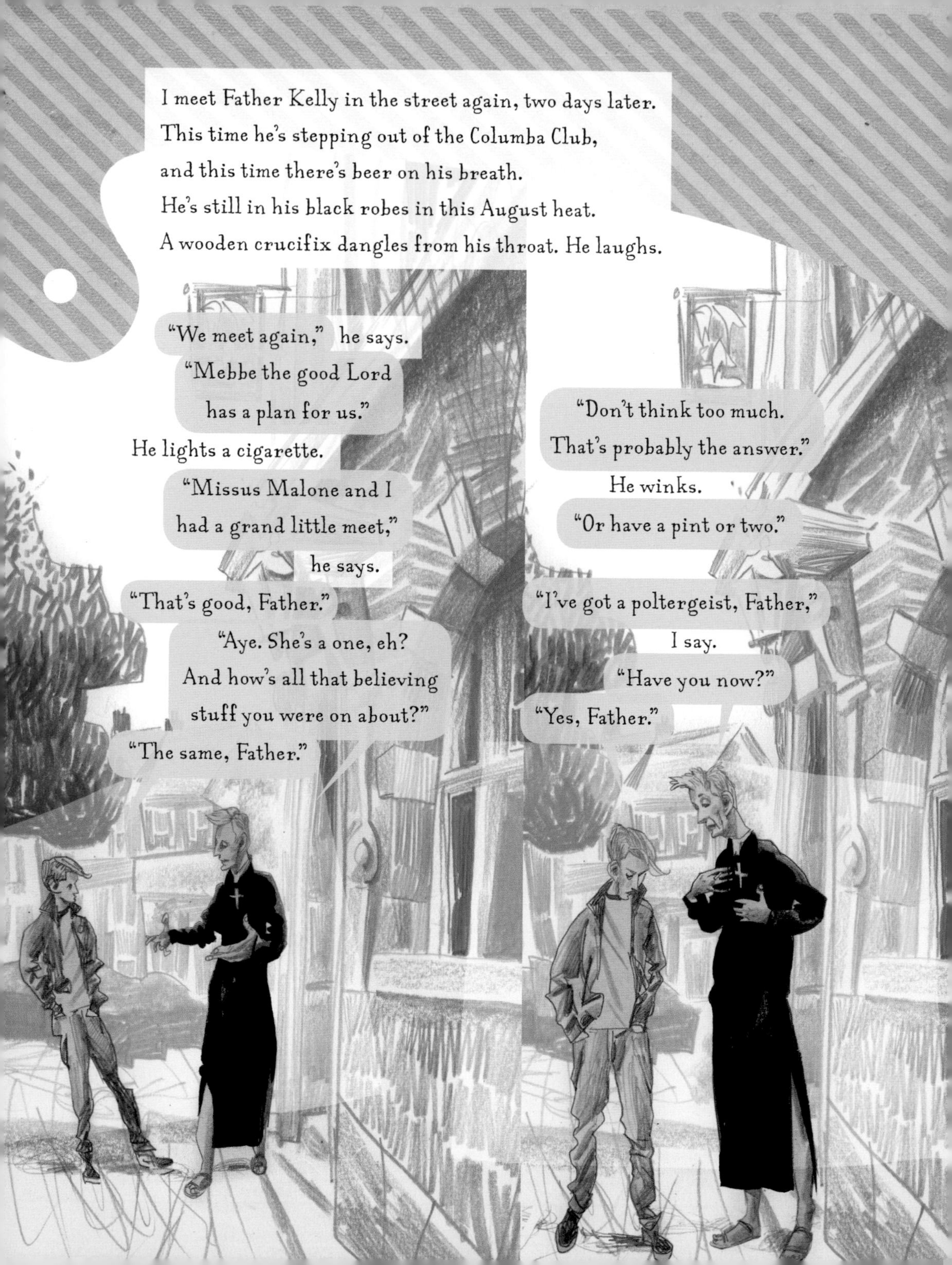
"We meet again," he says.
"Mebbe the good Lord has a plan for us."
He lights a cigarette.
"Missus Malone and I had a grand little meet,"
he says.
"That's good, Father."
"Aye. She's a one, eh? And how's all that believing stuff you were on about?"
"The same, Father."
"Don't think too much. That's probably the answer."
He winks.
"Or have a pint or two."
"I've got a poltergeist, Father,"
I say.
"Have you now?"
"Yes, Father."

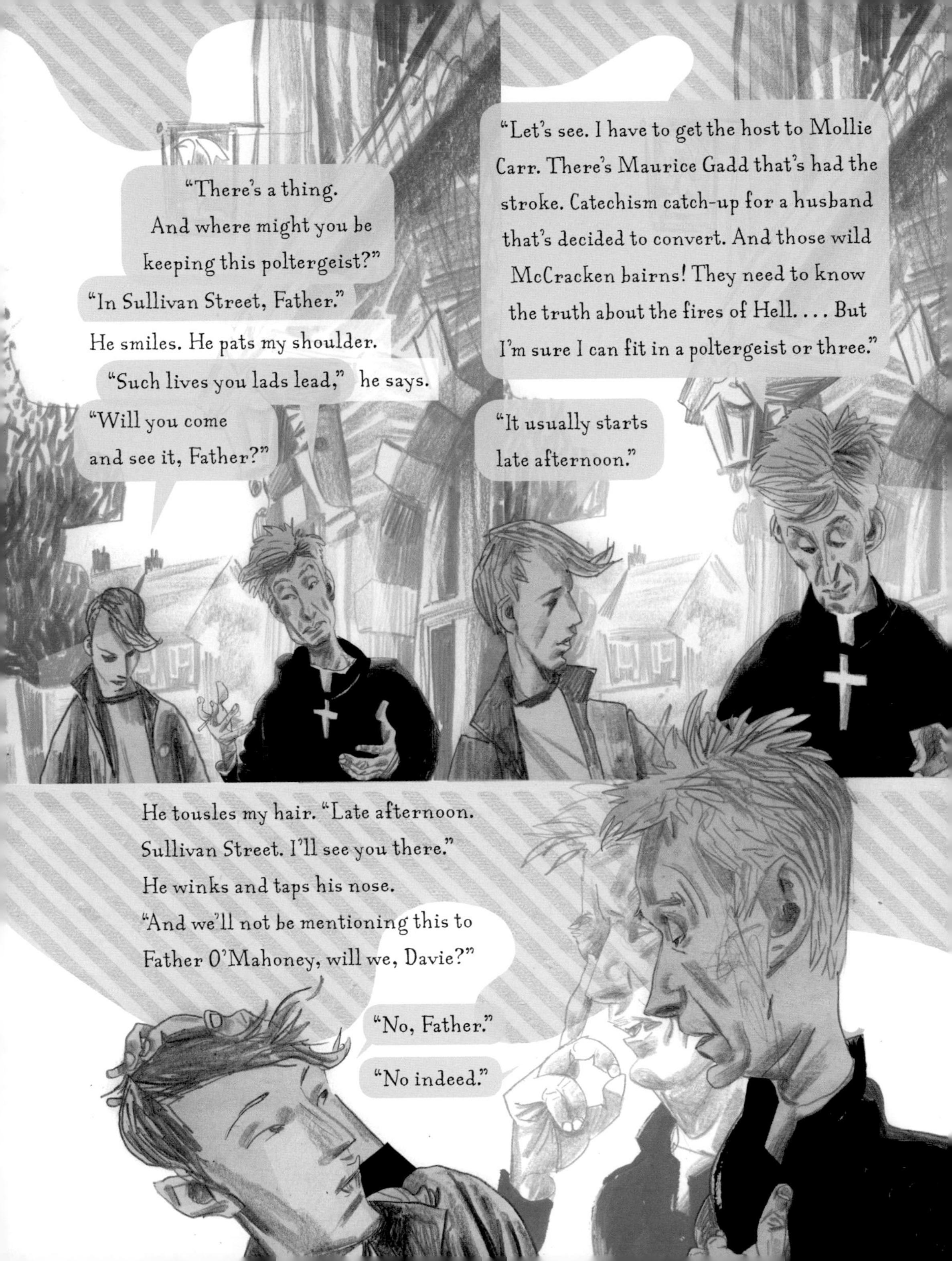
"There's a thing. And where might you be keeping this poltergeist?"
"In Sullivan Street, Father."
He smiles. He pats my shoulder.
"Such lives you lads lead," he says.
"Will you come and see it, Father?"
"Let's see. I have to get the host to Mollie Carr. There's Maurice Gadd that's had the stroke. Catechism catch-up for a husband that's decided to convert. And those wild McCracken bairns! They need to know the truth about the fires of Hell. . . . But I'm sure I can fit in a poltergeist or three."
"It usually starts late afternoon."
He tousles my hair. "Late afternoon. Sullivan Street. I'll see you there."
He winks and taps his nose.
"And we'll not be mentioning this to Father O'Mahoney, will we, Davie?"
"No, Father."
"No indeed."

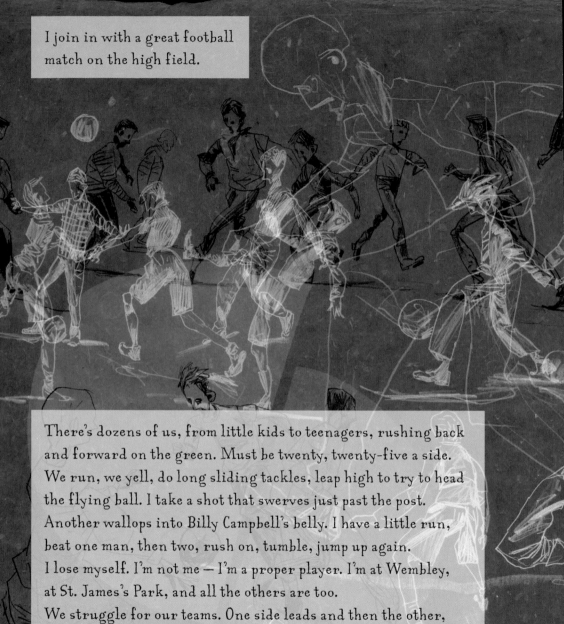

I join in with a great football
match on the high field.

There's dozens of us, from little kids to teenagers, rushing back
and forward on the green. Must be twenty, twenty-five a side.
We run, we yell, do long sliding tackles, leap high to try to head
the flying ball. I take a shot that swerves just past the post.
Another wallops into Billy Campbell's belly. I have a little run,
beat one man, then two, rush on, tumble, jump up again.
I lose myself. I'm not me — I'm a proper player. I'm at Wembley,
at St. James's Park, and all the others are too.
We struggle for our teams. One side leads and then the other,
then the first fights back again. In dashing through the field and
playing with the ball we change ourselves, we change the world.
Our muscles ache, our hearts thump, our lungs are fit to burst.

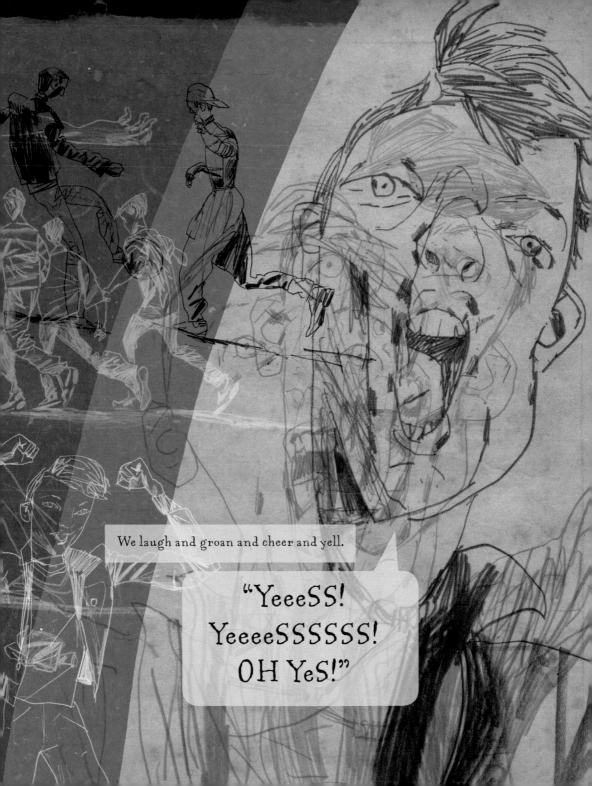

We laugh and groan and cheer and yell.

"YeeeSS! YeeeeSSSSSS! OH YeS!"

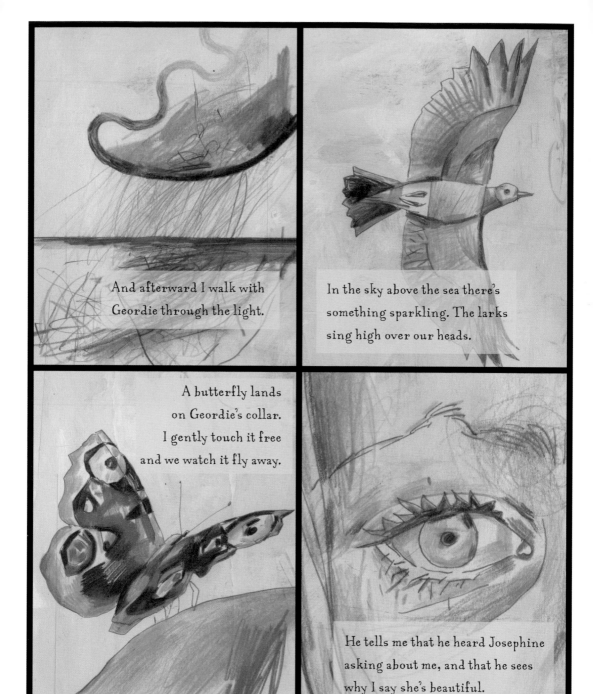

And afterward I walk with Geordie through the light.

In the sky above the sea there's something sparkling. The larks sing high over our heads.

A butterfly lands on Geordie's collar. I gently touch it free and we watch it fly away.

He tells me that he heard Josephine asking about me, and that he sees why I say she's beautiful.

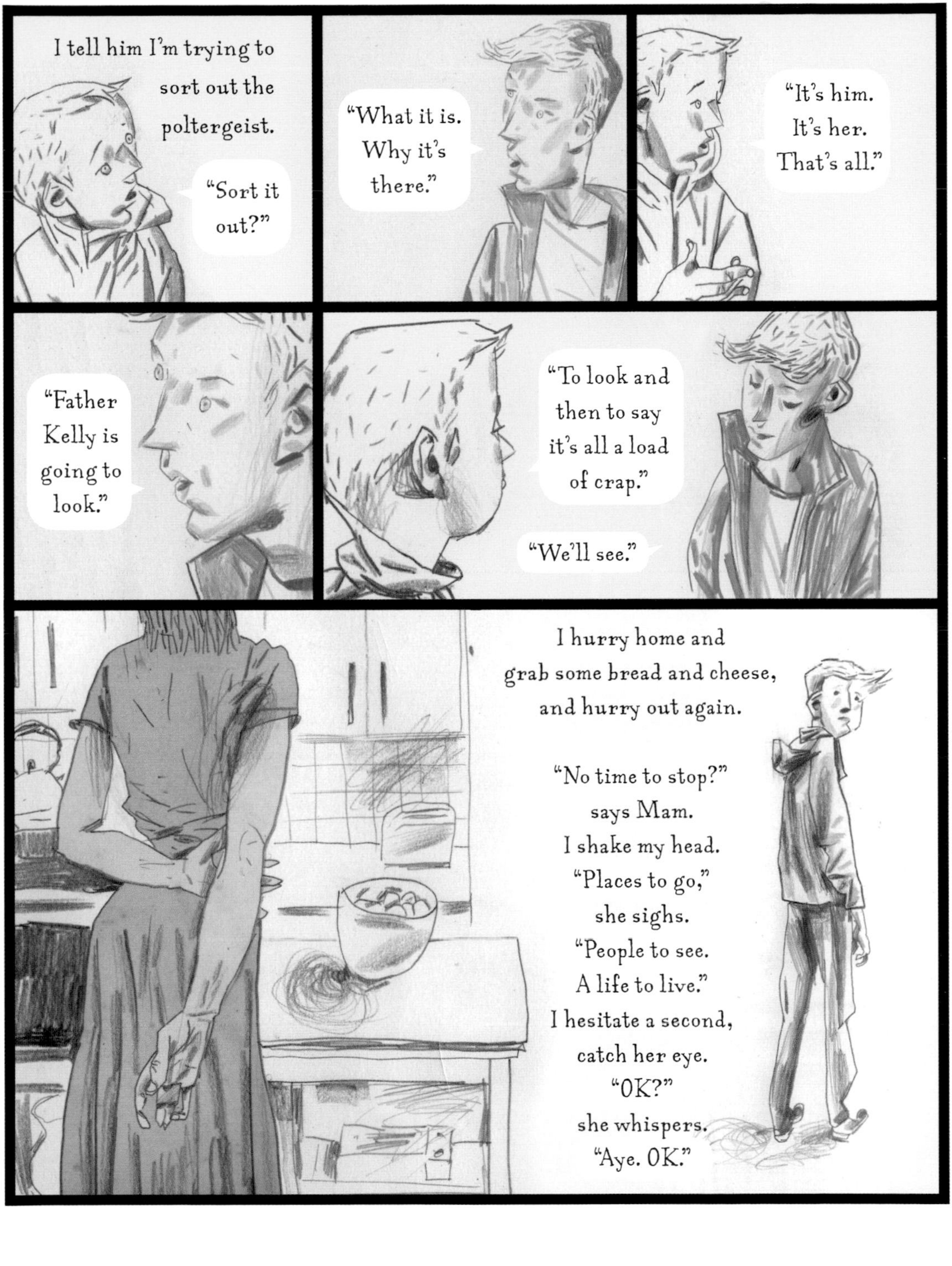

I tell him I'm trying to sort out the poltergeist.
"Sort it out?"
"What it is. Why it's there."
"It's him. It's her. That's all."
"Father Kelly is going to look."
"To look and then to say it's all a load of crap."
"We'll see."
I hurry home and grab some bread and cheese, and hurry out again.
"No time to stop?" says Mam. I shake my head. "Places to go," she sighs. "People to see. A life to live." I hesitate a second, catch her eye. "OK?" she whispers. "Aye. OK."

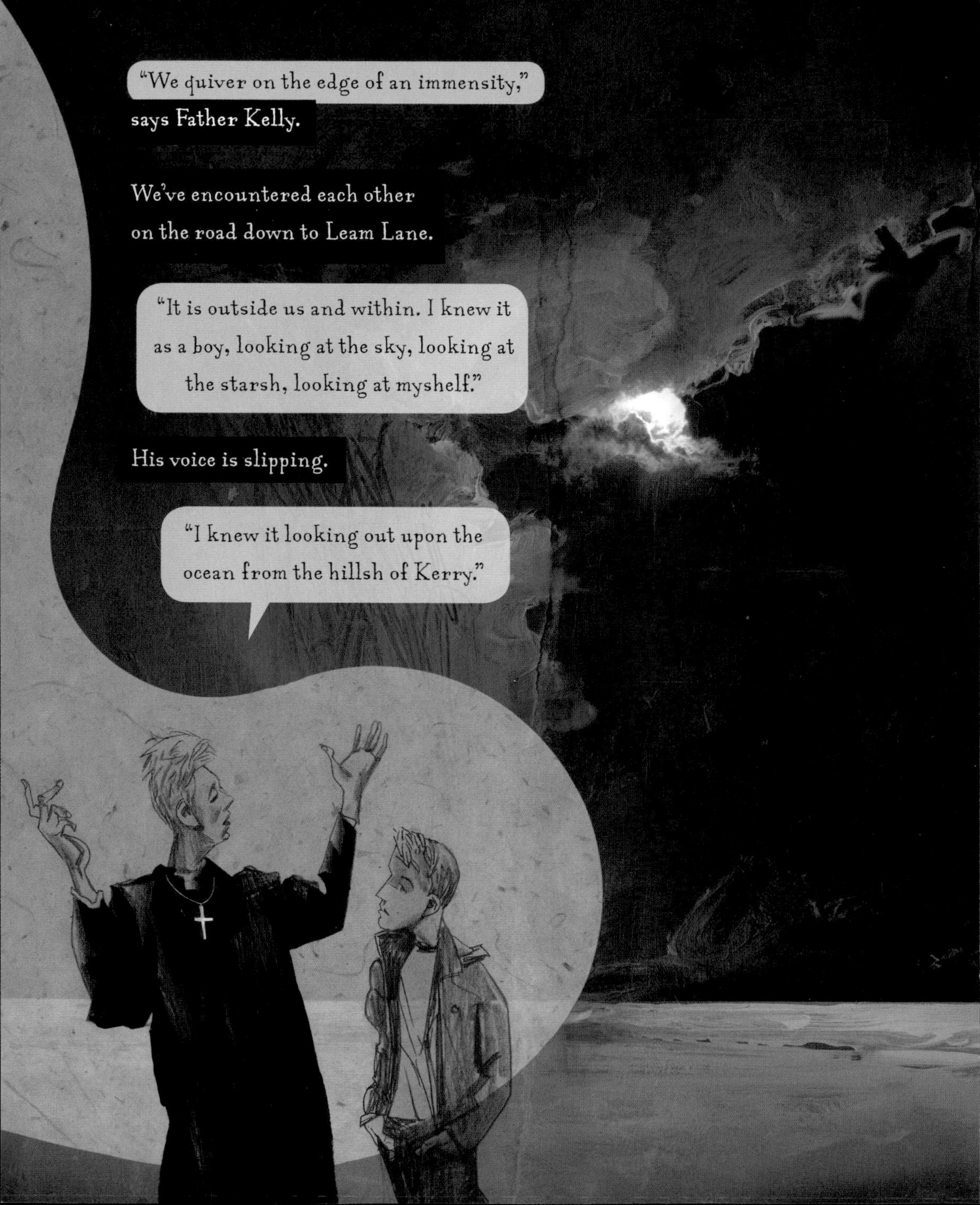
"We quiver on the edge of an immensity,"
says Father Kelly.
We've encountered each other on the road down to Leam Lane.
"It is outside us and within. I knew it as a boy, looking at the sky, looking at the starsh, looking at myshelf."
His voice is slipping.
"I knew it looking out upon the ocean from the hillsh of Kerry."

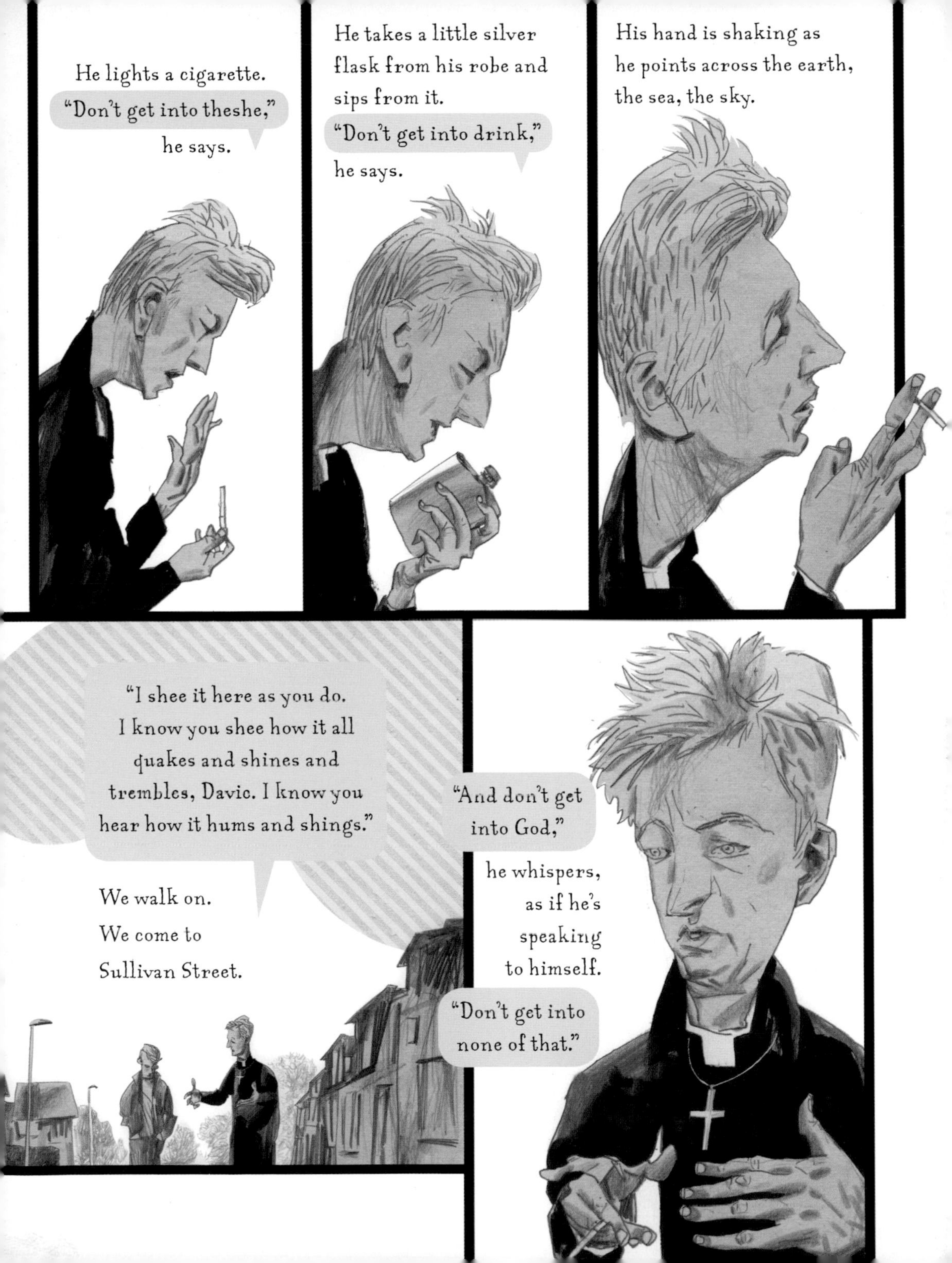
He lights a cigarette.
“Don’t get into theshe,”
he says.
He takes a little silver flask from his robe and sips from it.
“Don’t get into drink,”
he says.
His hand is shaking as he points across the earth, the sea, the sky.
“I shee it here as you do. I know you shee how it all quakes and shines and trembles, Davie. I know you hear how it hums and shings.”
We walk on. We come to Sullivan Street.
“And don’t get into God,”
he whispers, as if he’s speaking to himself.
“Don’t get into none of that.”

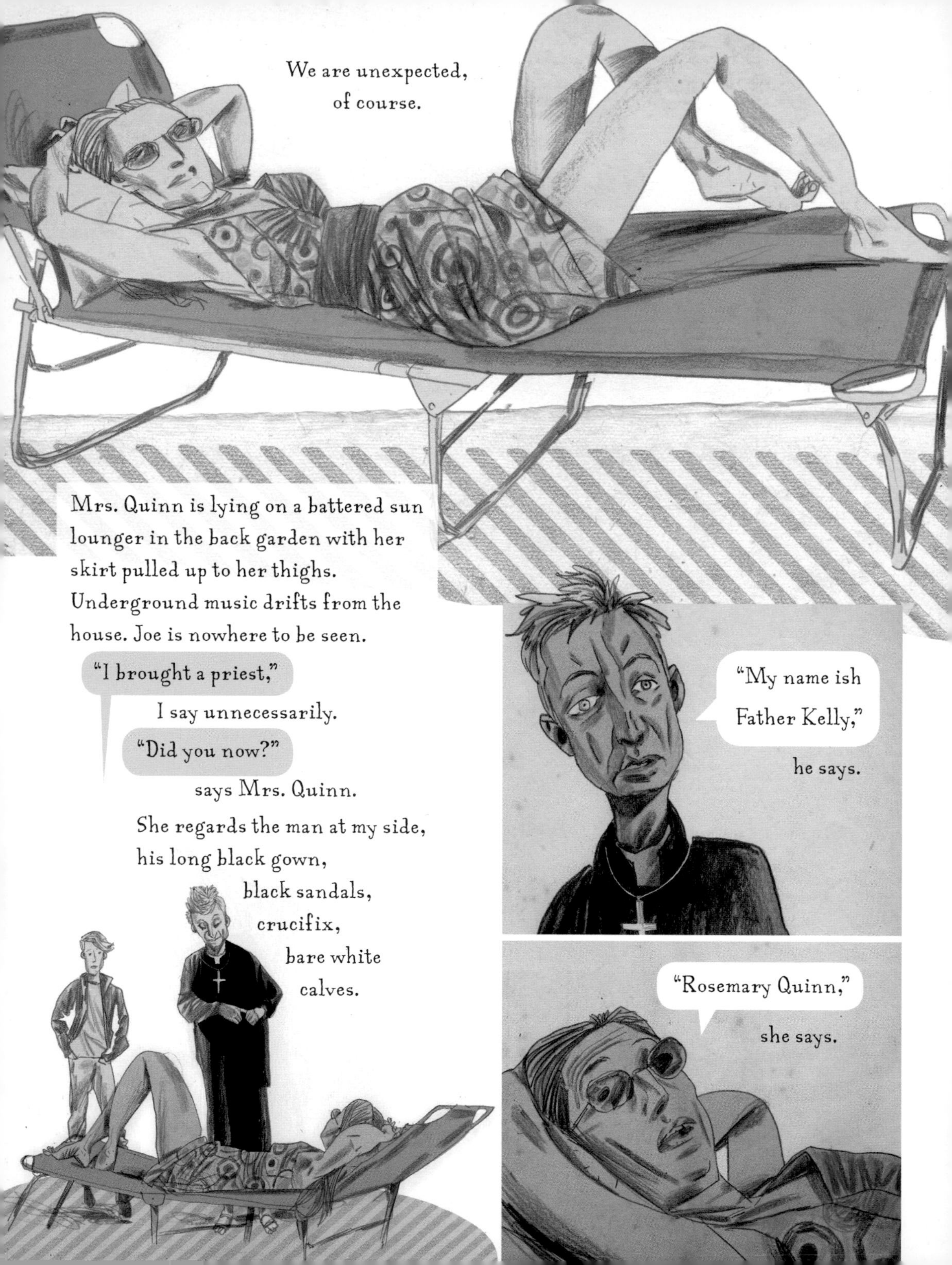
We are unexpected, of course.
Mrs. Quinn is lying on a battered sun lounger in the back garden with her skirt pulled up to her thighs. Underground music drifts from the house. Joe is nowhere to be seen.
"I brought a priest,"
I say unnecessarily.
"Did you now?"
says Mrs. Quinn.
She regards the man at my side, his long black gown, black sandals, crucifix, bare white calves.
"My name ish Father Kelly,"
he says.
"Rosemary Quinn,"
she says.

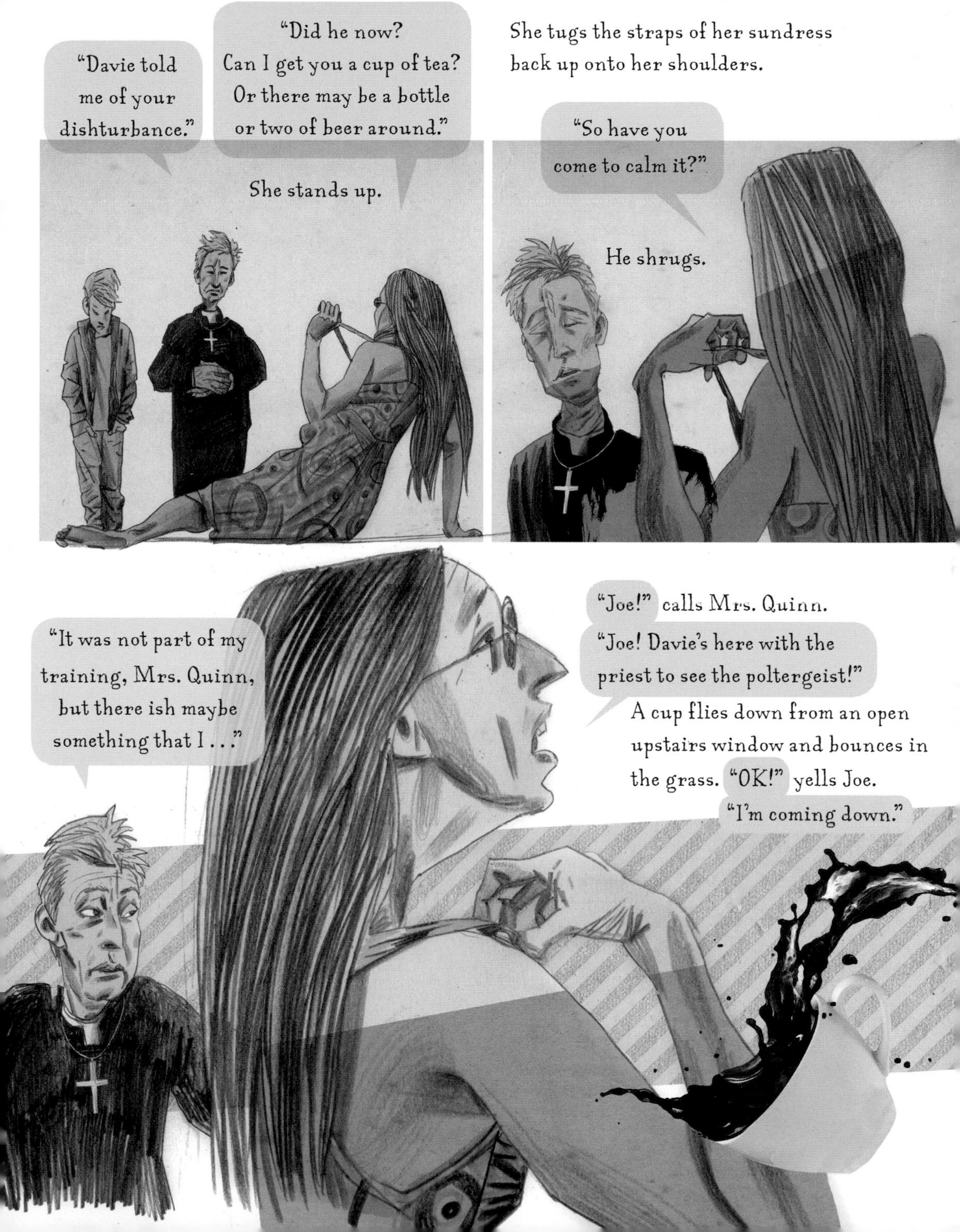
"Davie told me of your dishturbance."
"Did he now? Can I get you a cup of tea? Or there may be a bottle or two of beer around."
She stands up.
She tugs the straps of her sundress back up onto her shoulders.
"So have you come to calm it?"
He shrugs.
"It was not part of my training, Mrs. Quinn, but there ish maybe something that I . . ."
"Joe!" calls Mrs. Quinn.
"Joe! Davie's here with the priest to see the poltergeist!"
A cup flies down from an open upstairs window and bounces in the grass. "OK!" yells Joe.
"I'm coming down."

Inside the kitchen, fragments of broken crockery lie against the baseboards. There's a new little jagged hole in one of the windows. Strips of wallpaper are curling from the walls. Joe comes downstairs with an orange bandage on his brow.

"And look at this," he says.

He lifts up a chair and shows that one of its legs has been ripped off.

"Just came down one morning and there it was like this," he says.

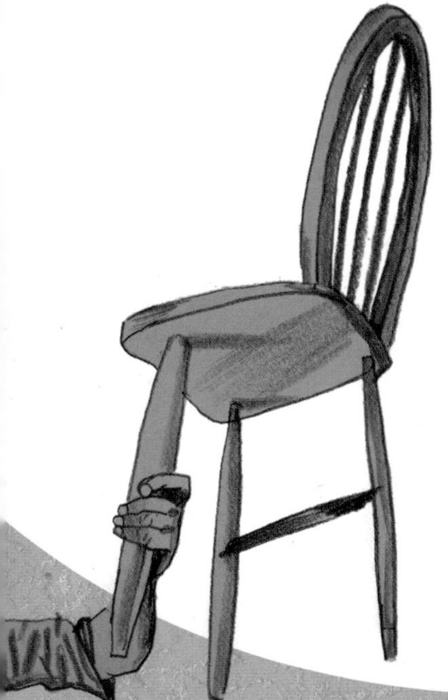

His mother stares at the priest.

"What is doing this?" she says.

"What are these strange forces?"

She holds out a bottle of beer and a glass to him.

He pours carefully.

He drinks.

She stands close,

leans up to him.

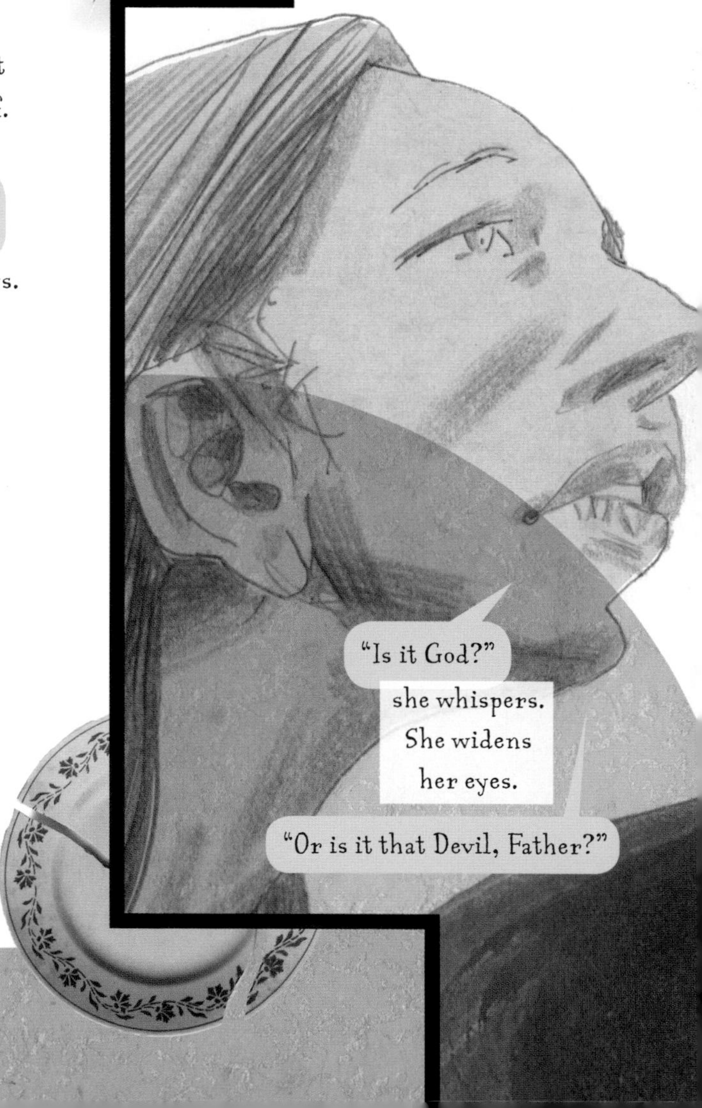

"Is it God?" she whispers. She widens her eyes. "Or is it that Devil, Father?"

A knife clatters against the wall. The priest flinches. He looks at Joe, at me. He drinks. There's a sound of something shattering upstairs.

We all stand silent, we listen and watch.
A dog howls.
The sun is sinking over the estate.
I am poised to be terrified, to be illuminated,
for the forces to work again.
For a while nothing more happens.
There's just stillness, silence and the immensity within and outside us. We all sigh.

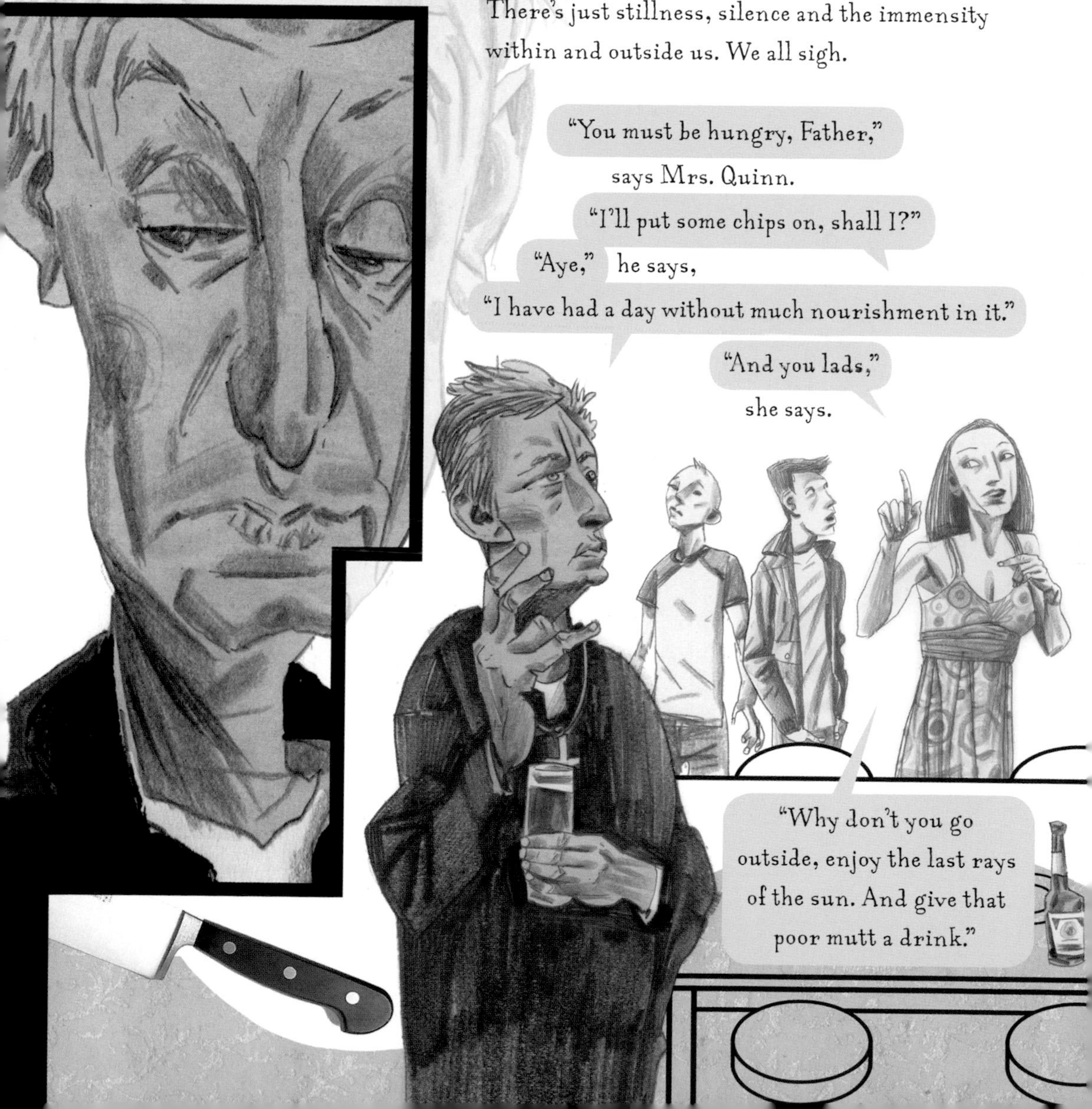
"You must be hungry, Father,"
says Mrs. Quinn.
"I'll put some chips on, shall I?"
"Aye,"
he says,
"I have had a day without much nourishment in it."
"And you lads,"
she says.
"Why don't you go outside, enjoy the last rays of the sun. And give that poor mutt a drink."

We do.
We perch on the edge of the sun lounger.
"Is it you?" I say.
"'Course it's not. In fact, according to me dad, it's him."
"What?"

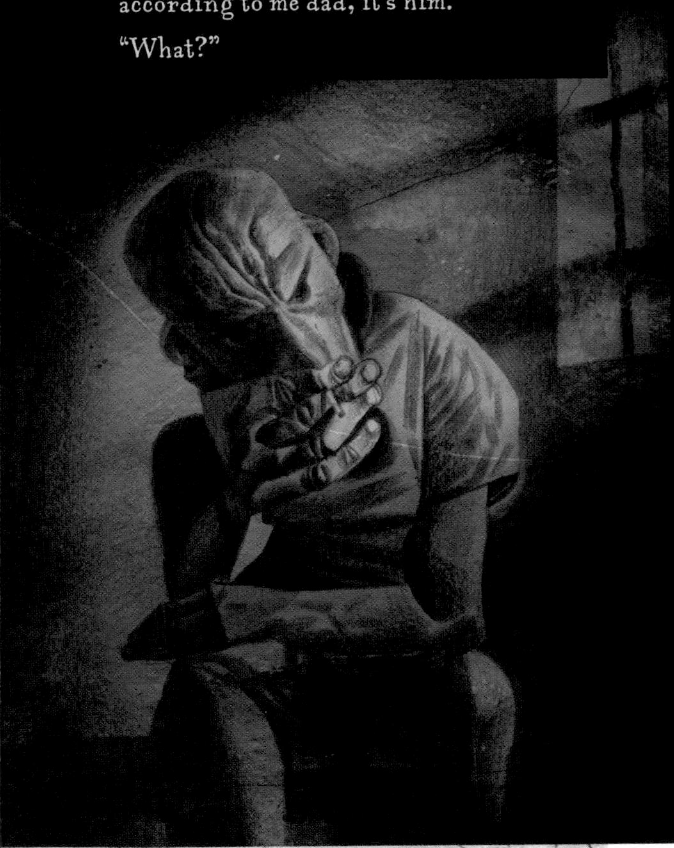

"We went to see him in jail on Sunday. What a bliddy nightmare place. He said he'd been focusing his thoughts on the house, making things move by the power of his will."
"What? Why?"
Joe holds out a packet of cigarettes to me. I don't take one.
He lights one for himself and blows the smoke across my face.
"I think he's mebbe trying to harm us," he says. "He's coming up with all these tales of what me mother's doing while he's inside. I think he's goin' bliddy mad, Davie.
You should see how wild his eyes are now. You should see how scared the officers are of him.
He's turnin' to a bliddy monster!
How's Josephine?"
"Eh?"

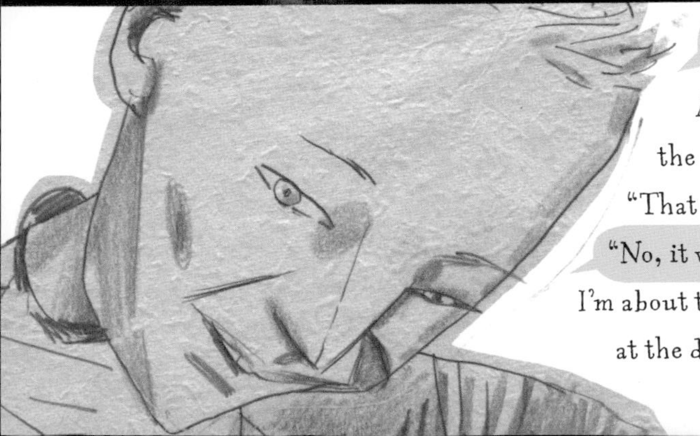

"You shagged her yet?"
A clod of earth flies up from the ground and over our heads.
"That was you!" I cry.
"No, it wasn't. Have you, eh?"
I'm about to go for him but his mother's at the door. The chips are done.

We go inside and sit at the little Formica table. Father Kelly's into the second bottle of beer. The air is golden through the broken window. The chips, the ketchup, and the bread are all delicious.

My mug of tea trembles as I lift it. It tilts and tea splashes down onto the tabletop. Mrs. Quinn puts her hand over mine.

"You OK, Davie?" she says.

"Aye."

Father Kelly smiles.

"The boy — like all boys — ish prey to great forces, great hungers, great emotionsh."

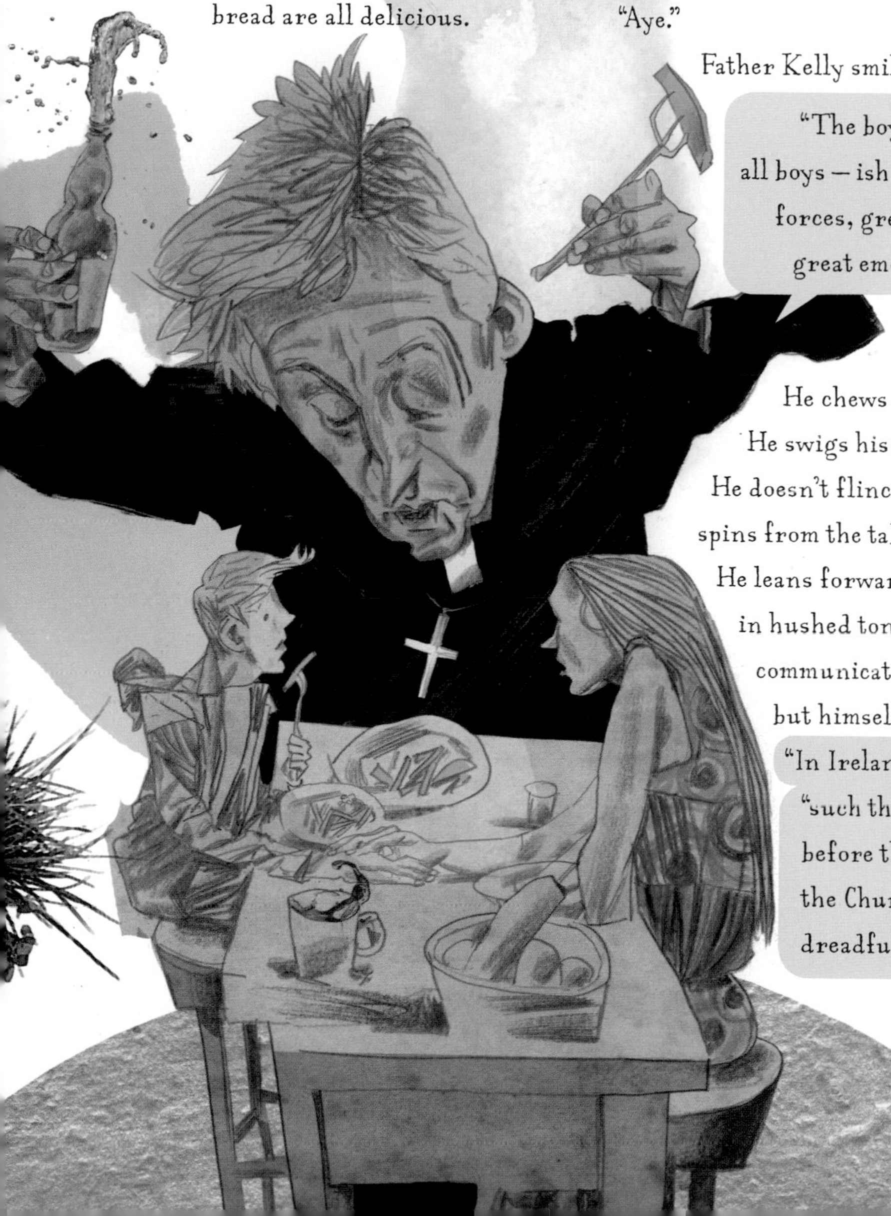

He chews his chips.

He swigs his beer.

He doesn't flinch as a plate spins from the table to the floor.

He leans forward and speaks in hushed tones, as if to communicate with nobody but himself.

"In Ireland," he says, "such things were known, before the dead hand of the Church took us in its dreadful grip."

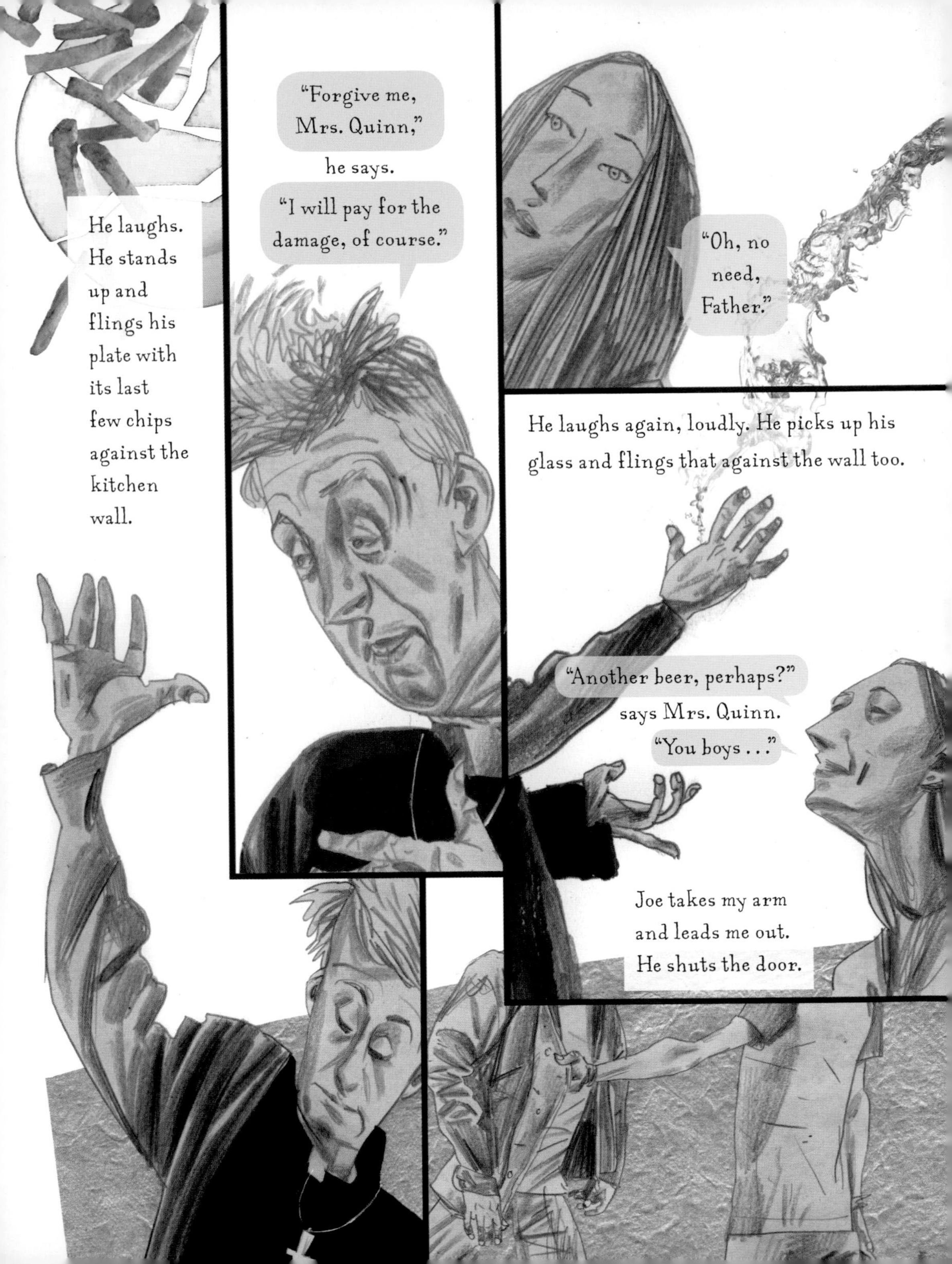
He laughs. He stands up and flings his plate with its last few chips against the kitchen wall.
"Forgive me, Mrs. Quinn,"
he says.
"I will pay for the damage, of course."
"Oh, no need, Father."
He laughs again, loudly. He picks up his glass and flings that against the wall too.
"Another beer, perhaps?"
says Mrs. Quinn.
"You boys . . ."
Joe takes my arm and leads me out. He shuts the door.

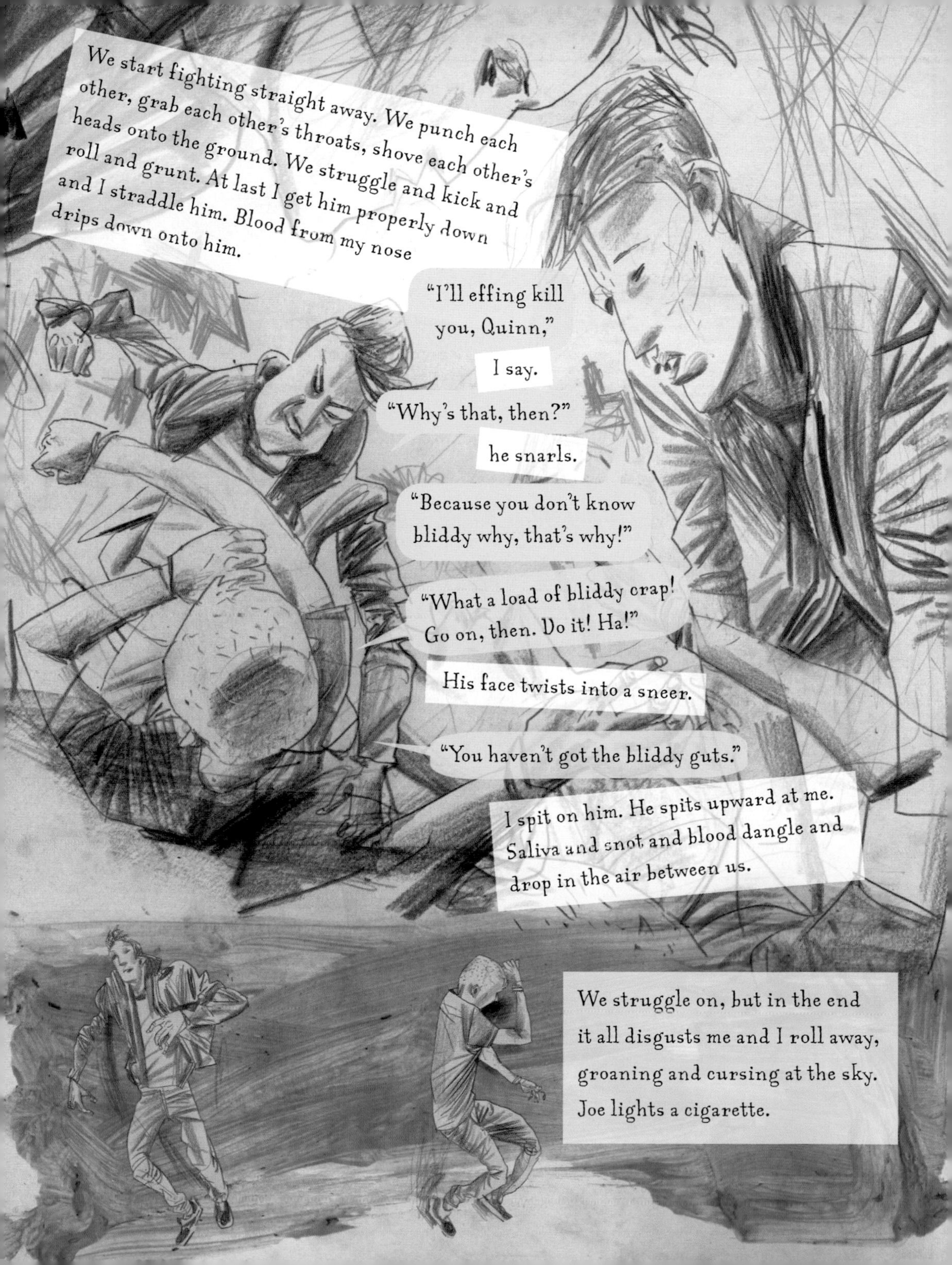
We start fighting straight away. We punch each other, grab each other's throats, shove each other's heads onto the ground. We struggle and kick and roll and grunt. At last I get him properly down and I straddle him. Blood from my nose drips down onto him.
"I'll effing kill you, Quinn,"
I say.
"Why's that, then?"
he snarls.
"Because you don't know bliddy why, that's why!"
"What a load of bliddy crap! Go on, then. Do it! Ha!"
His face twists into a sneer.
"You haven't got the bliddy guts."
I spit on him. He spits upward at me. Saliva and snot and blood dangle and drop in the air between us.
We struggle on, but in the end it all disgusts me and I roll away, groaning and cursing at the sky. Joe lights a cigarette.

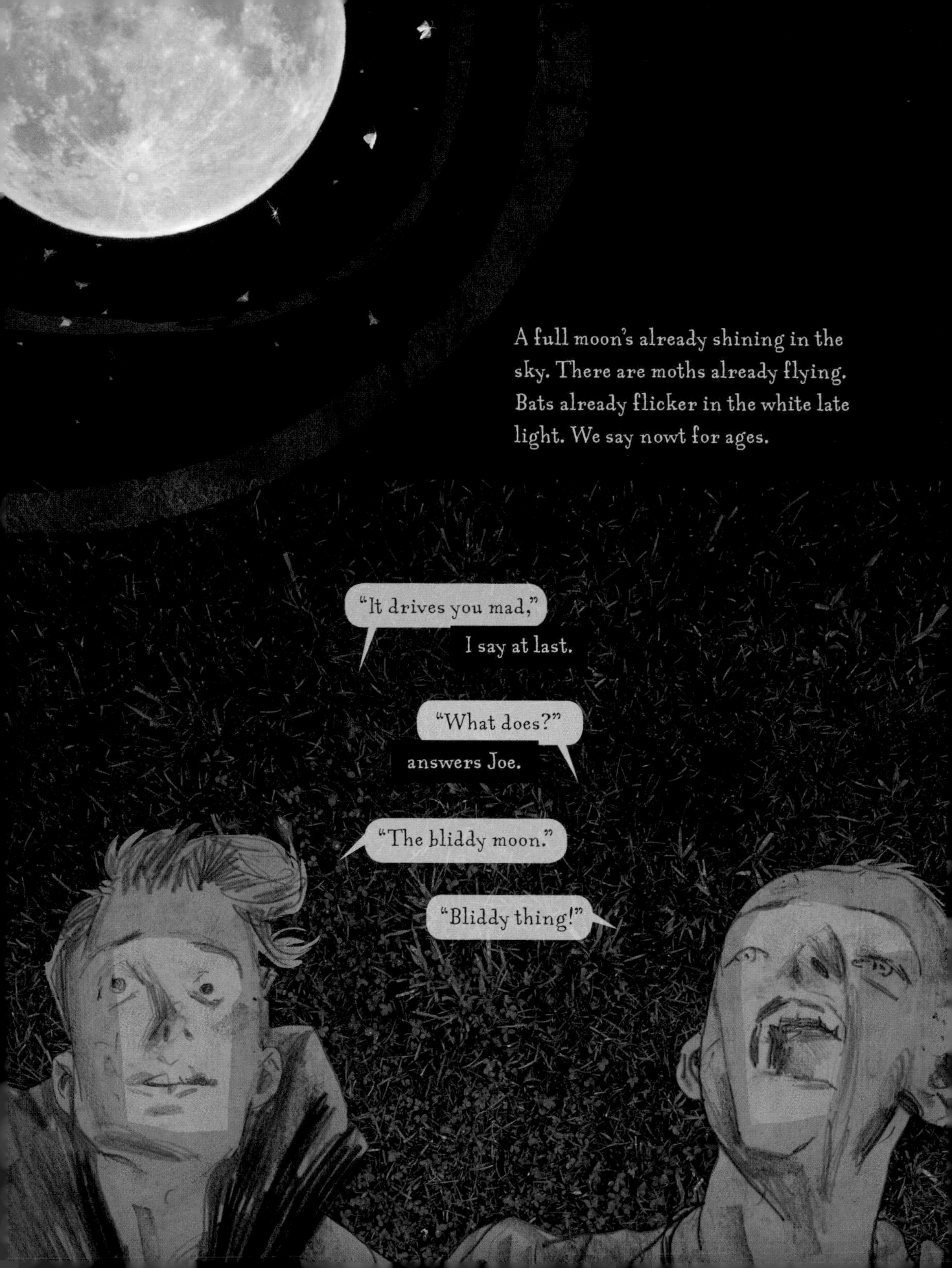
A full moon's already shining in the sky. There are moths already flying. Bats already flicker in the white late light. We say nowt for ages.
"It drives you mad,"
I say at last.
"What does?"
answers Joe.
"The bliddy moon."
"Bliddy thing!"

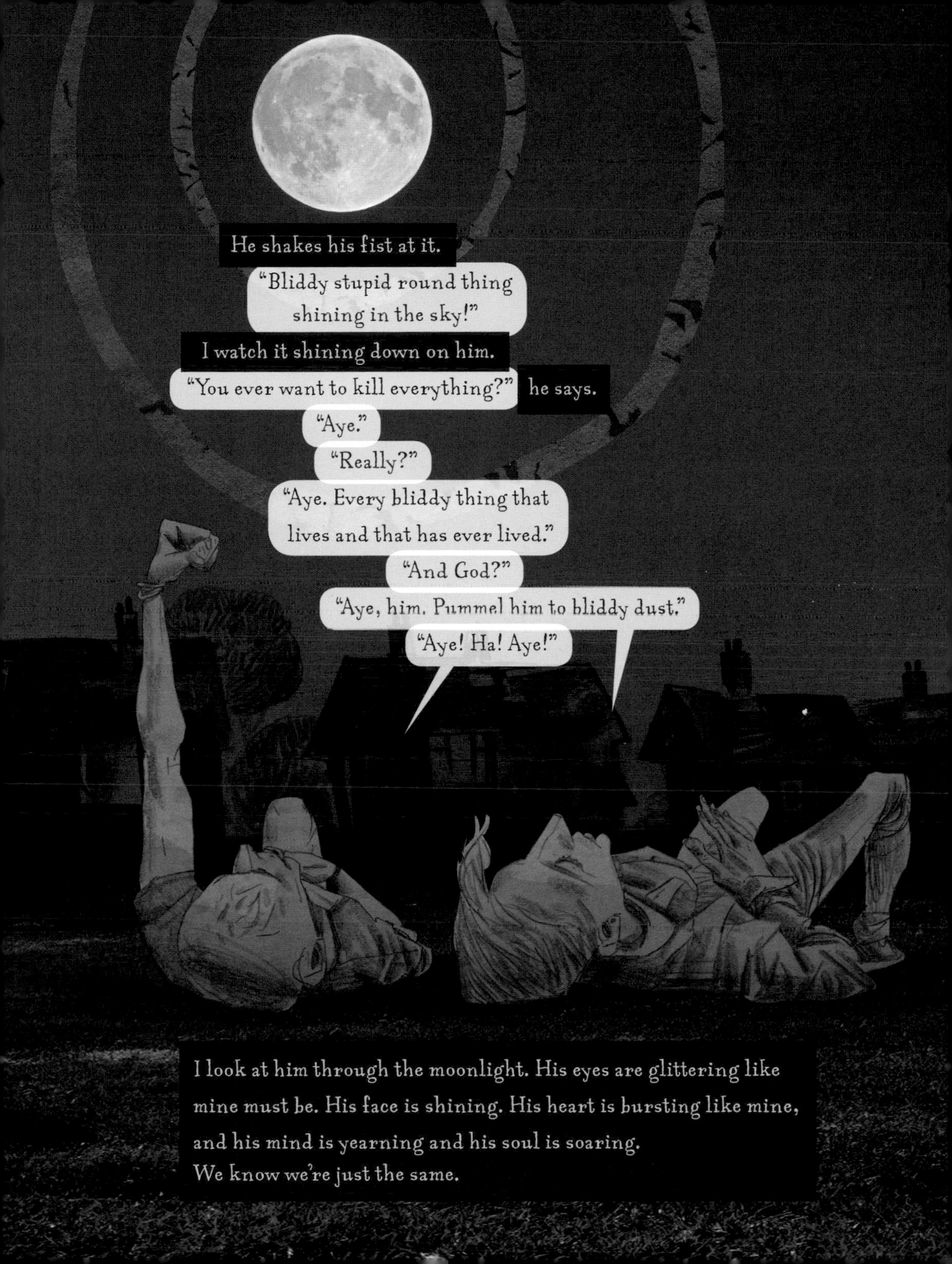
He shakes his fist at it.
"Bliddy stupid round thing shining in the sky!"
I watch it shining down on him.
"You ever want to kill everything?" he says.
"Aye."
"Really?"
"Aye. Every bliddy thing that lives and that has ever lived."
"And God?"
"Aye, him. Pummel him to bliddy dust."
"Aye! Ha! Aye!"
I look at him through the moonlight. His eyes are glittering like mine must be. His face is shining. His heart is bursting like mine, and his mind is yearning and his soul is soaring.
We know we're just the same.

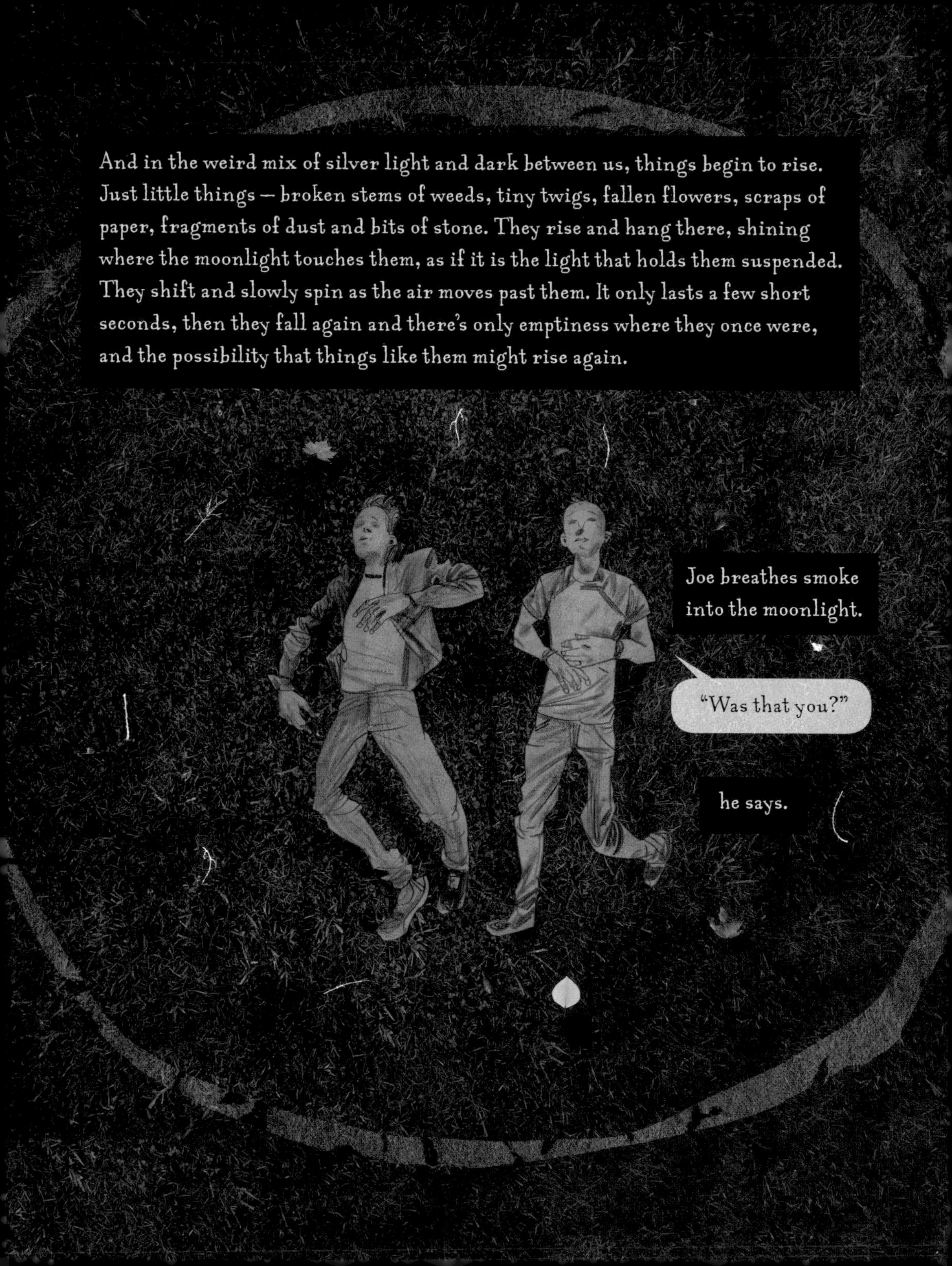
And in the weird mix of silver light and dark between us, things begin to rise. Just little things — broken stems of weeds, tiny twigs, fallen flowers, scraps of paper, fragments of dust and bits of stone. They rise and hang there, shining where the moonlight touches them, as if it is the light that holds them suspended. They shift and slowly spin as the air moves past them. It only lasts a few short seconds, then they fall again and there's only emptiness where they once were, and the possibility that things like them might rise again.
Joe breathes smoke into the moonlight.
"Was that you?"
he says.

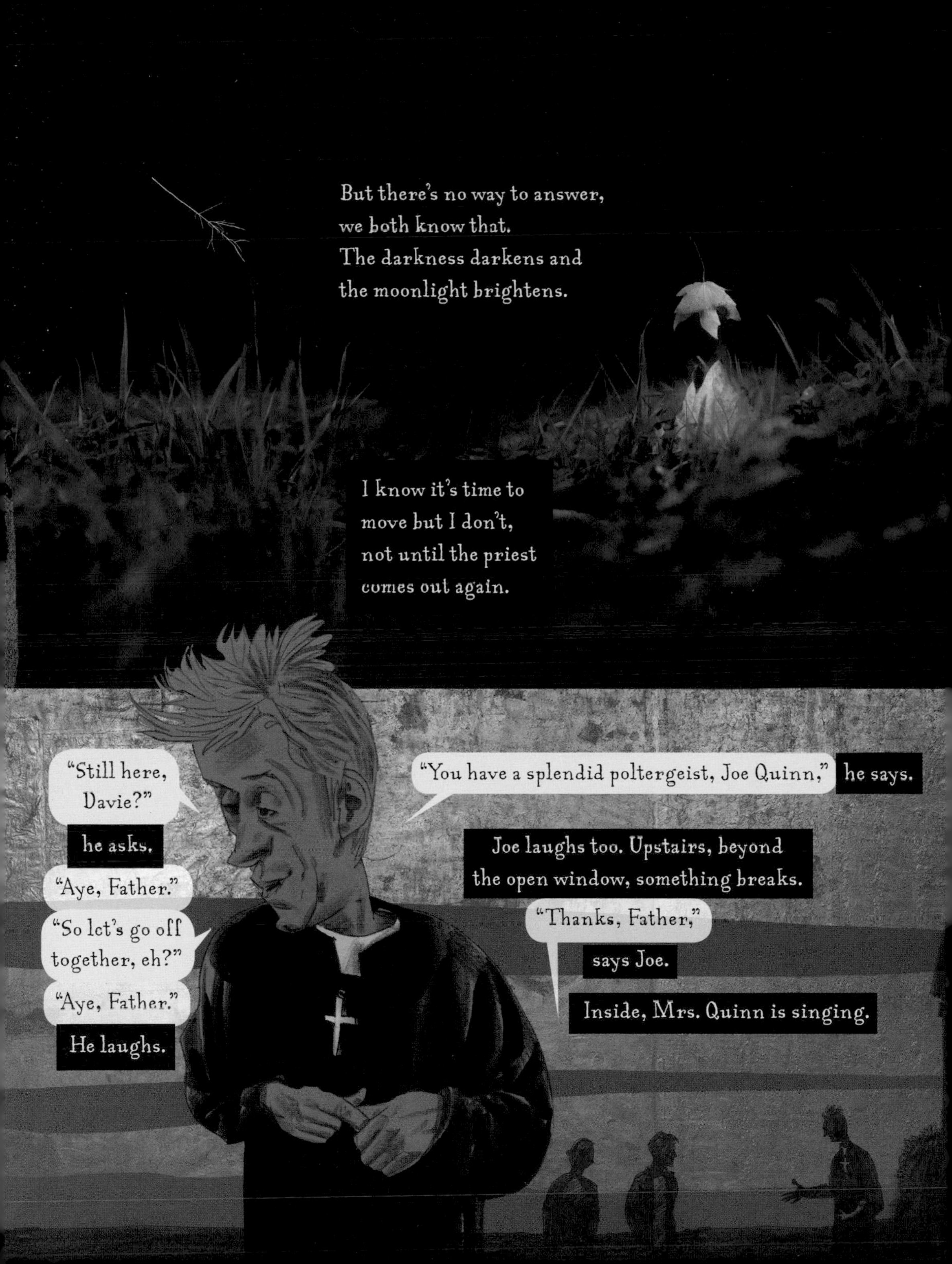

But there's no way to answer,
we both know that.
The darkness darkens and
the moonlight brightens.
I know it's time to
move but I don't,
not until the priest
comes out again.
"Still here, Davie?"
he asks.
"Aye, Father."
"So let's go off together, eh?"
"Aye, Father."
He laughs.
"You have a splendid poltergeist, Joe Quinn,"
he says.
Joe laughs too. Upstairs, beyond
the open window, something breaks.
"Thanks, Father,"
says Joe.
Inside, Mrs. Quinn is singing.

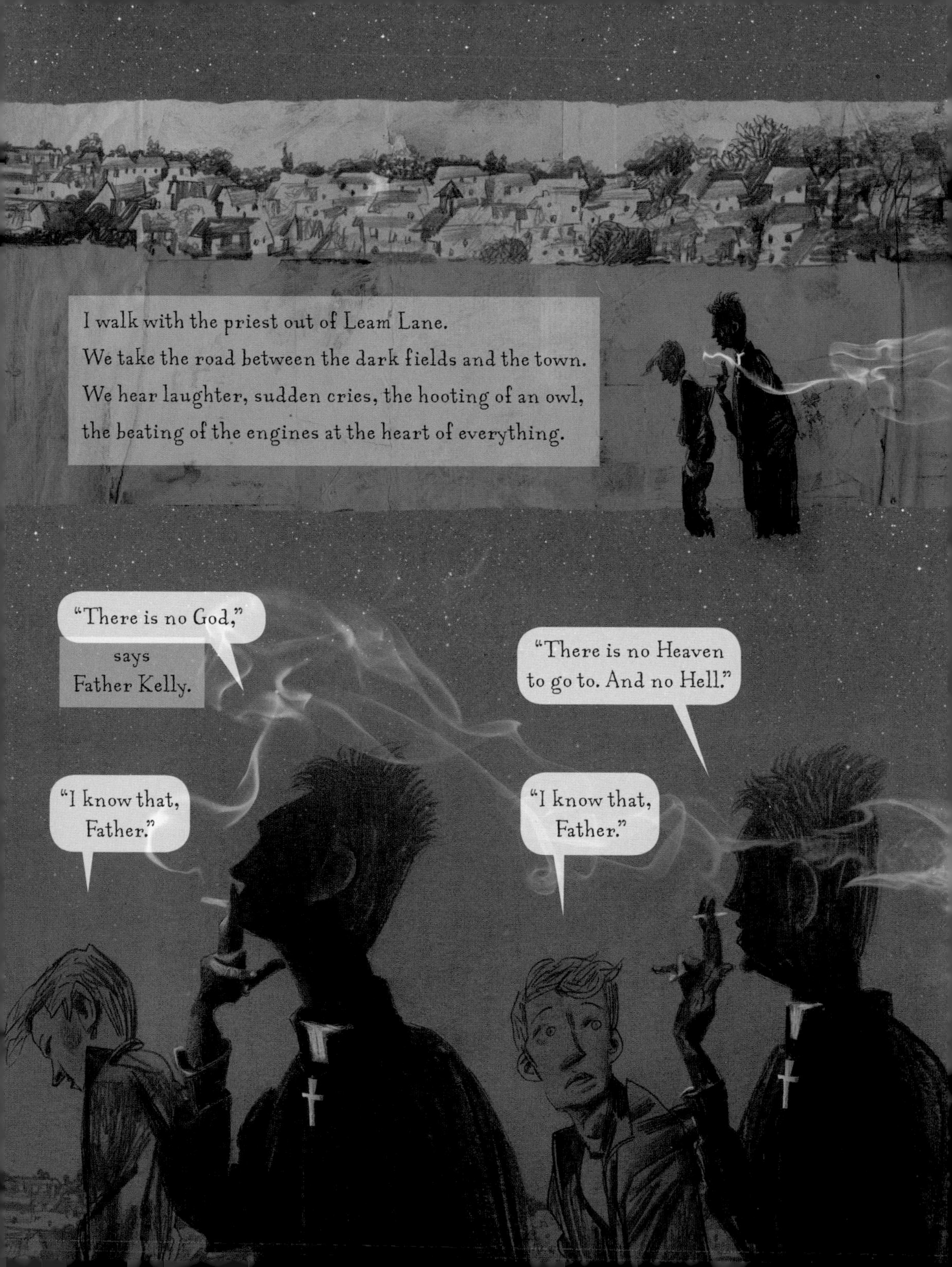
I walk with the priest out of Leam Lane.
We take the road between the dark fields and the town.
We hear laughter, sudden cries, the hooting of an owl,
the beating of the engines at the heart of everything.
"There is no God,"
says Father Kelly.
"There is no Heaven to go to. And no Hell."
"I know that, Father."
"I know that, Father."

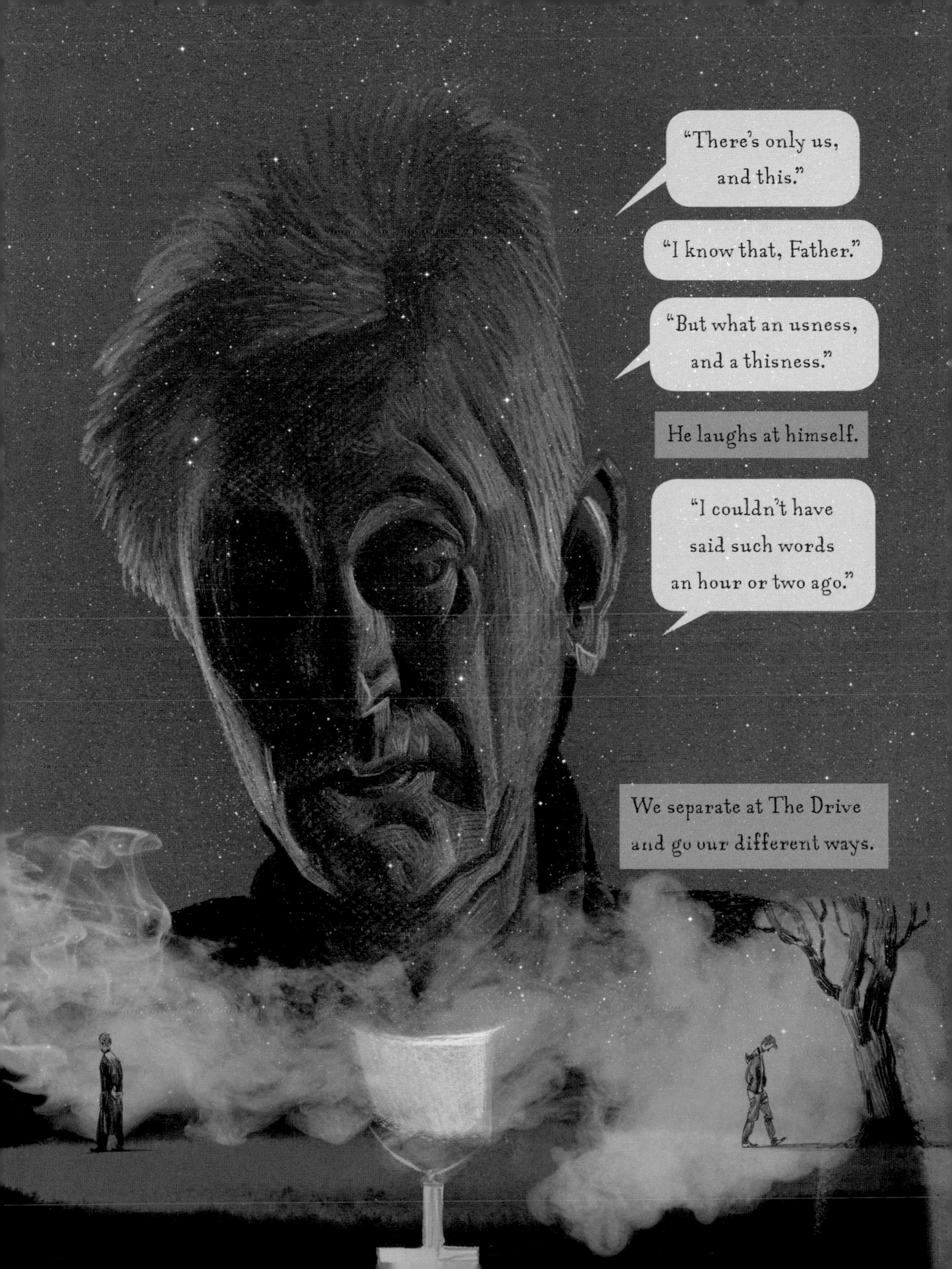
"There's only us, and this."
"I know that, Father."
"But what an usness, and a thisness."
He laughs at himself.
"I couldn't have said such words an hour or two ago."
We separate at The Drive and go our different ways.

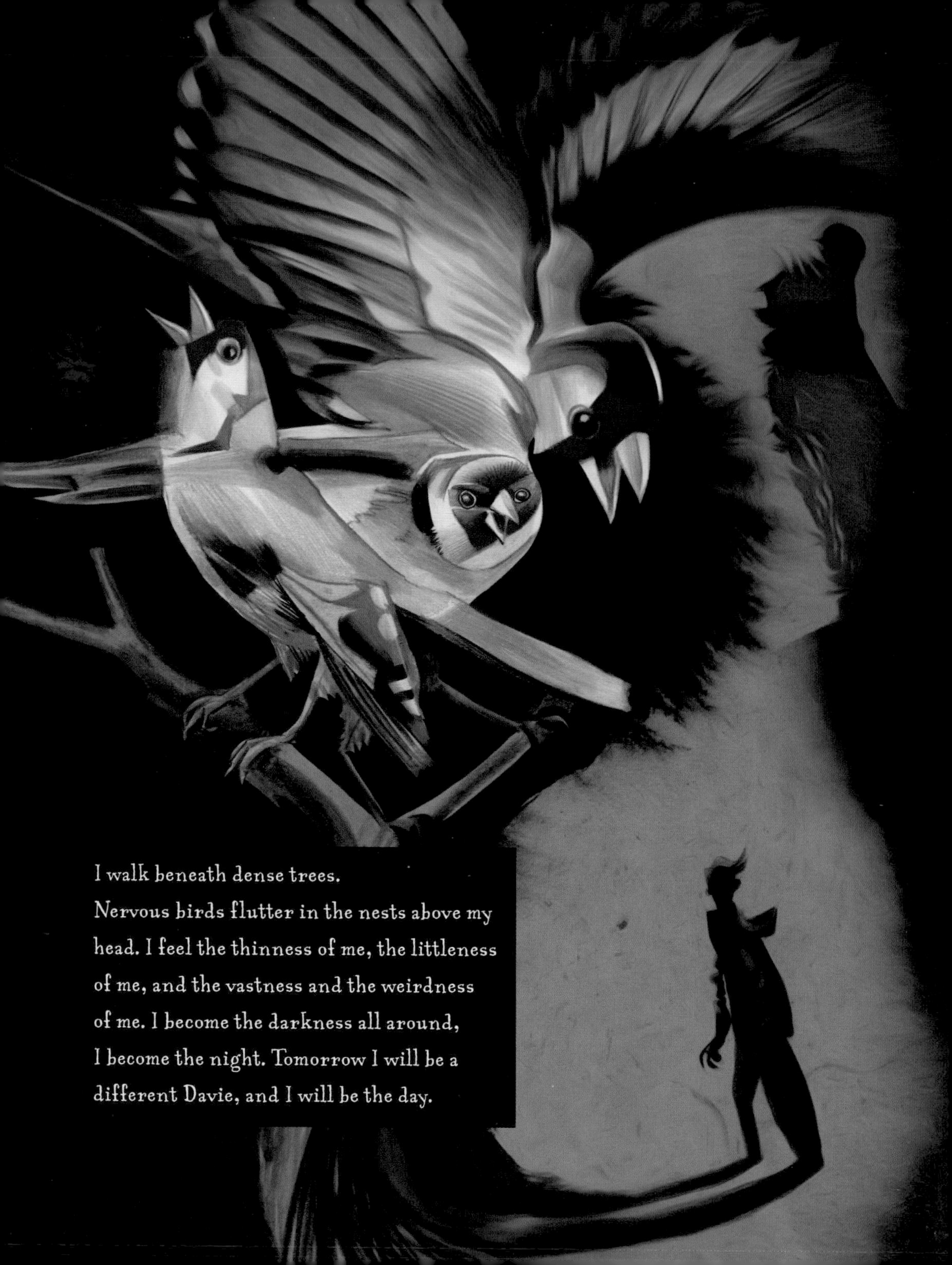

I walk beneath dense trees.
Nervous birds flutter in the nests above my head. I feel the thinness of me, the littleness of me, and the vastness and the weirdness of me. I become the darkness all around, I become the night. Tomorrow I will be a different Davie, and I will be the day.

Suddenly I know
the poltergeist is me.
It is in me.

It is me in fury at Joe Quinn,
me in love with Josephine,
me in hatred of the nonexistent God. It
is me in dread and bliddy grief,
it is me in wonder at this place,
this earth, this moon,
this night.

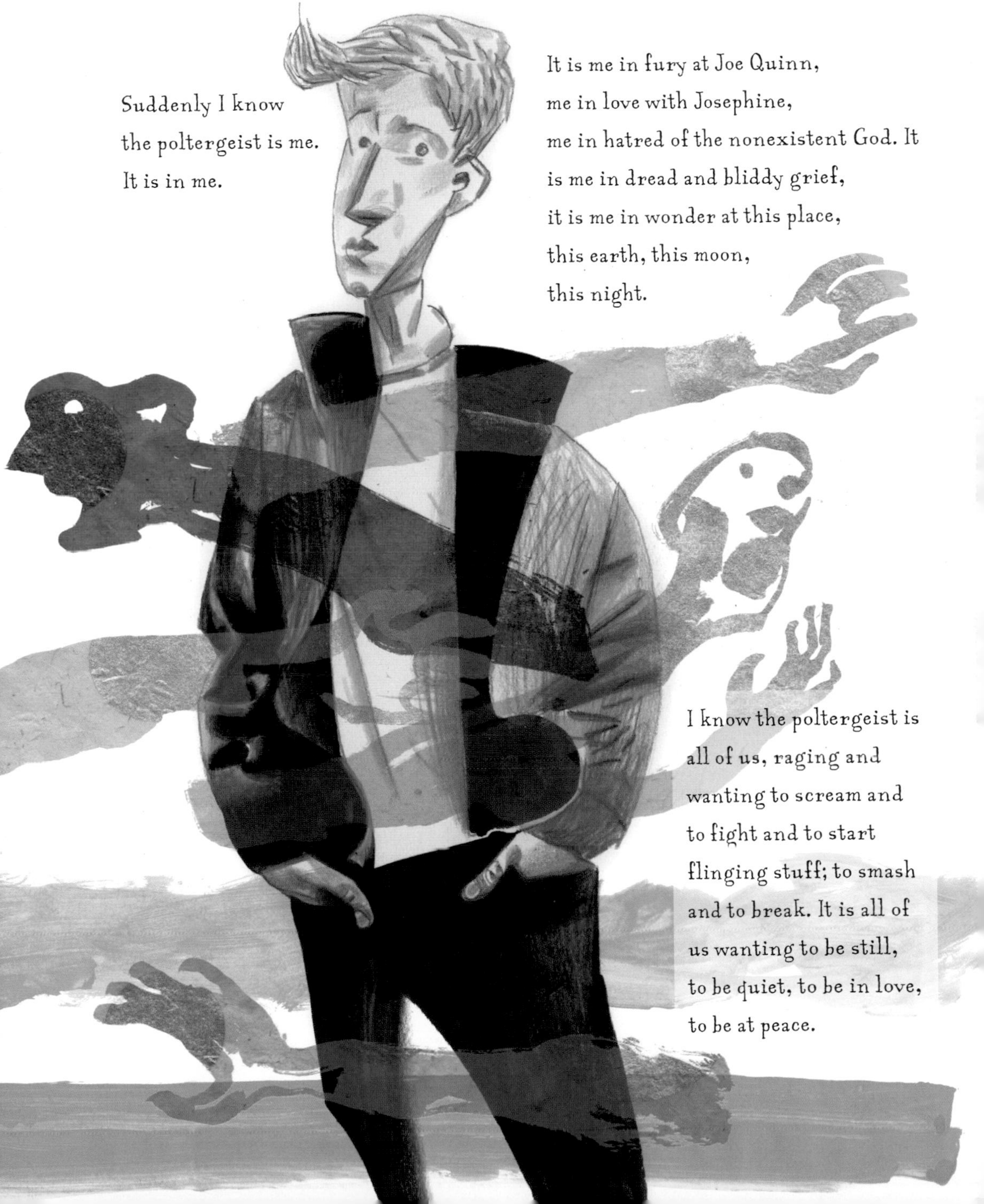

I know the poltergeist is
all of us, raging and
wanting to scream and
to fight and to start
flinging stuff; to smash
and to break. It is all of
us wanting to be still,
to be quiet, to be in love,
to be at peace.

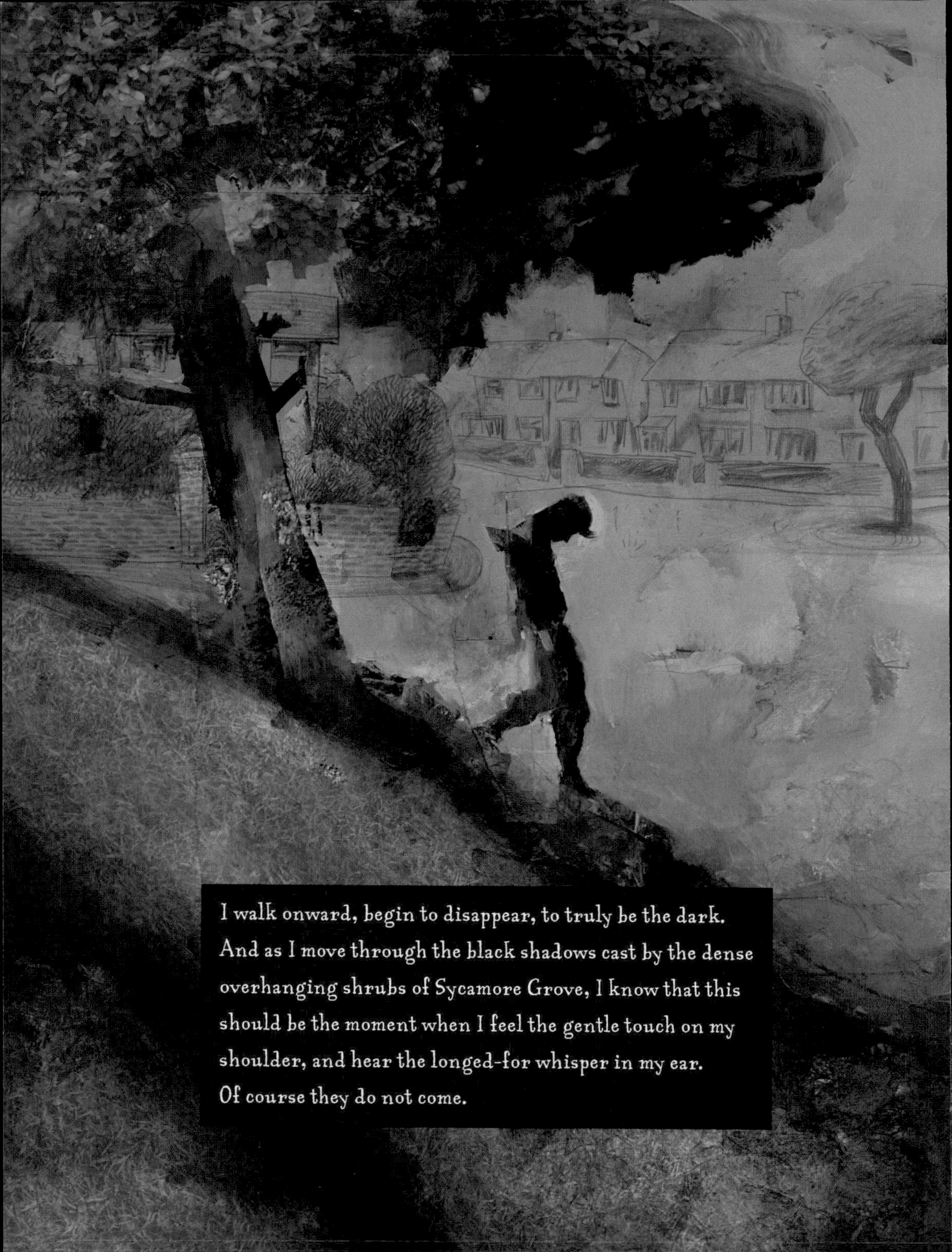

I walk onward, begin to disappear, to truly be the dark. And as I move through the black shadows cast by the dense overhanging shrubs of Sycamore Grove, I know that this should be the moment when I feel the gentle touch on my shoulder, and hear the longed-for whisper in my ear. Of course they do not come.

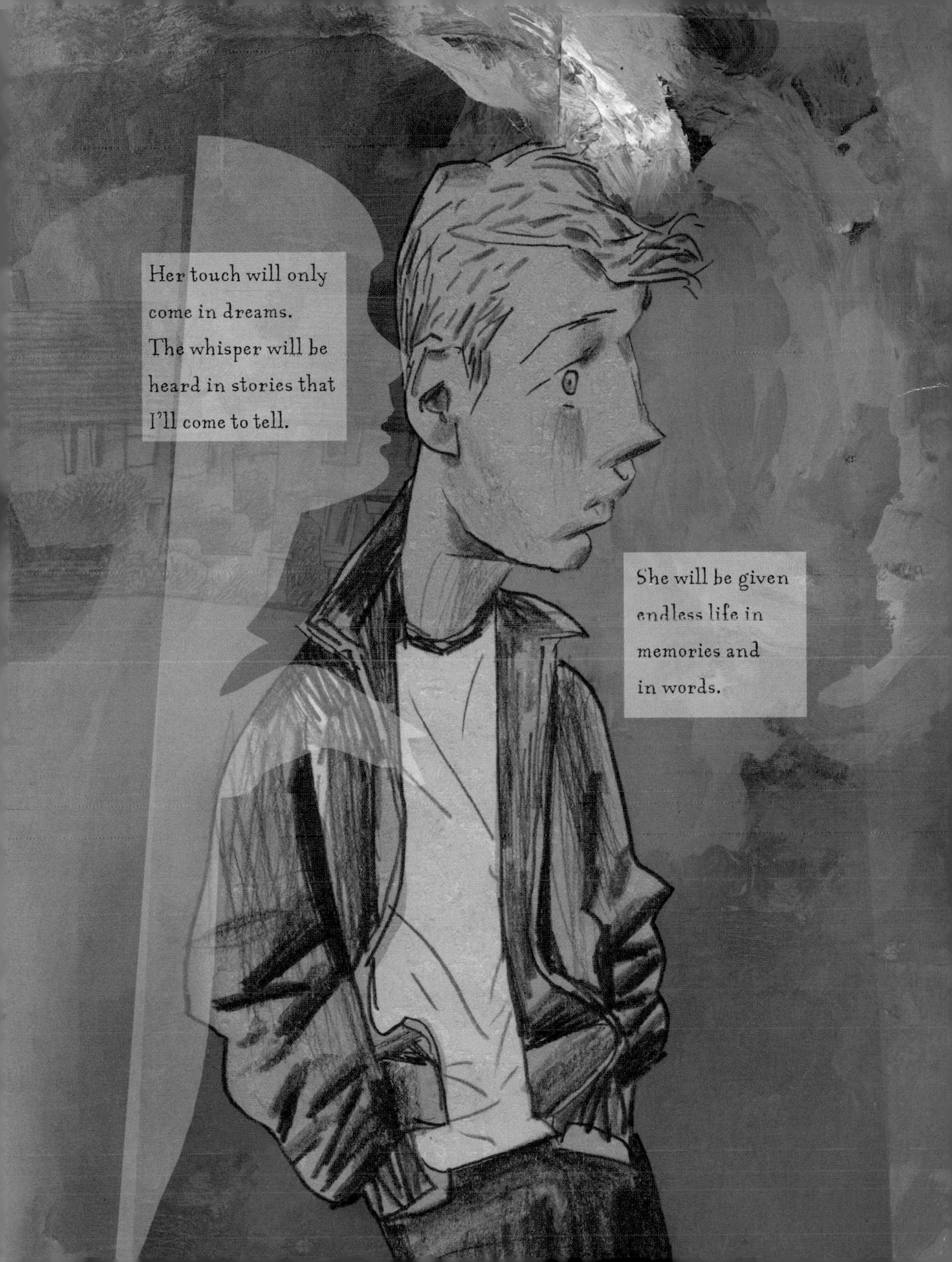
Her touch will only come in dreams. The whisper will be heard in stories that I'll come to tell.
She will be given endless life in memories and in words.

I walk on below the streetlights toward the square, toward my home.
Tomorrow I'll play football with Geordie and the lads on the high fields.

Soon I will kiss Josephine Minto
beneath the cherry tree in Holly Hill Park.

Father Kelly will return to Ireland, where he will be unfrocked.

Mr. Quinn will kill a cellmate and will stay in jail.
Joe Quinn's poltergeist will disappear.

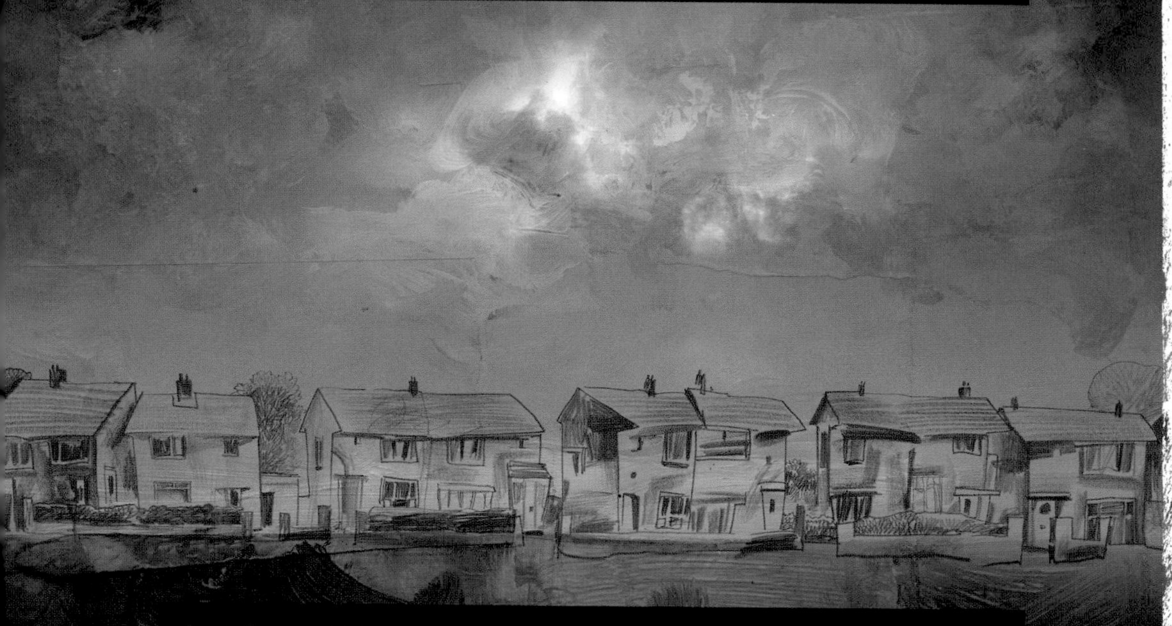

And there will be other occurrences, an immensity of them,
and the world and all that's in it will continue to hum and sing,
to shake and shine, to hold us in its darkness and its light.

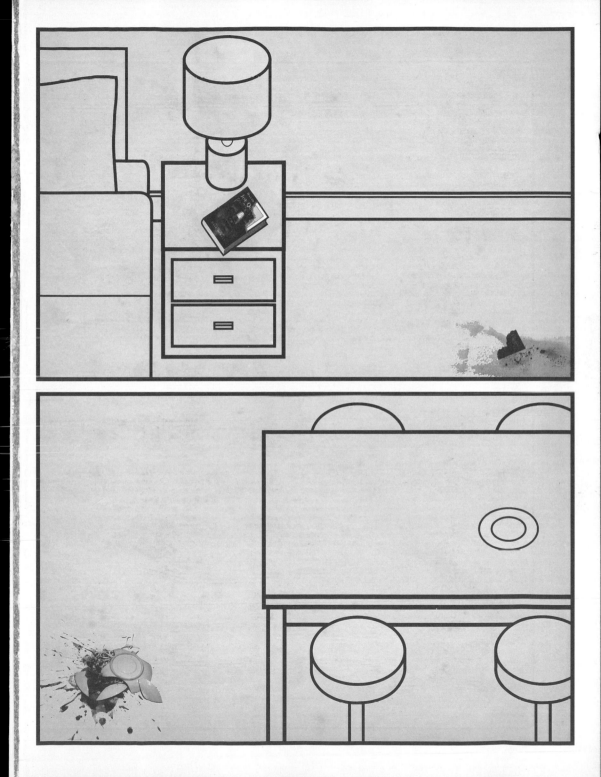

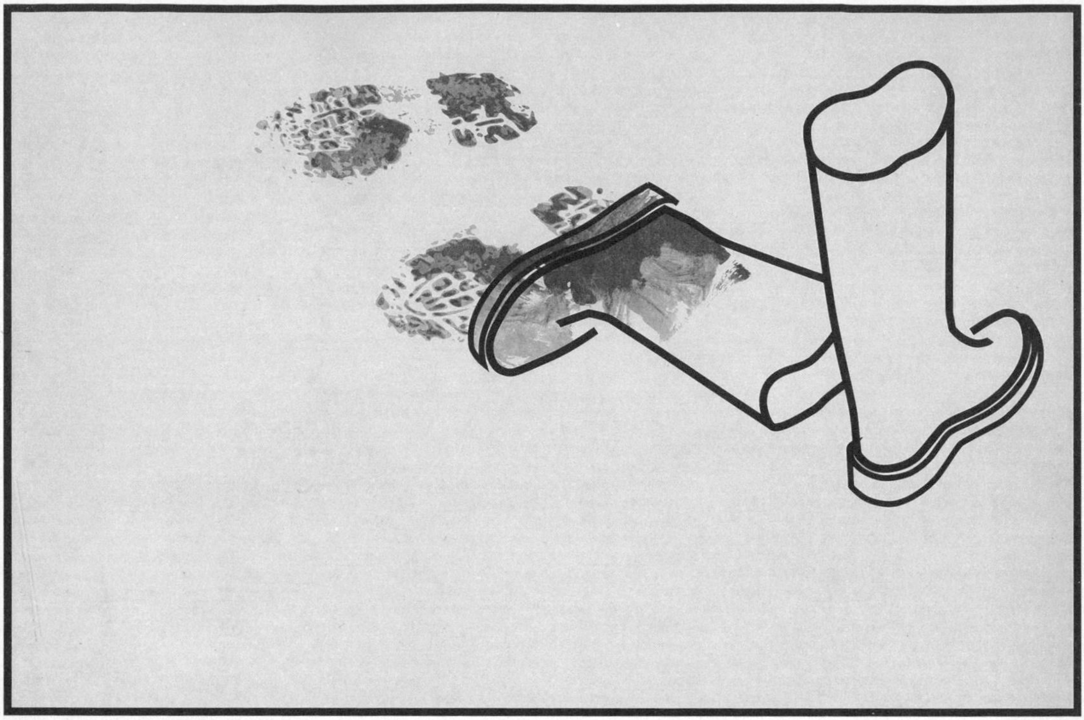
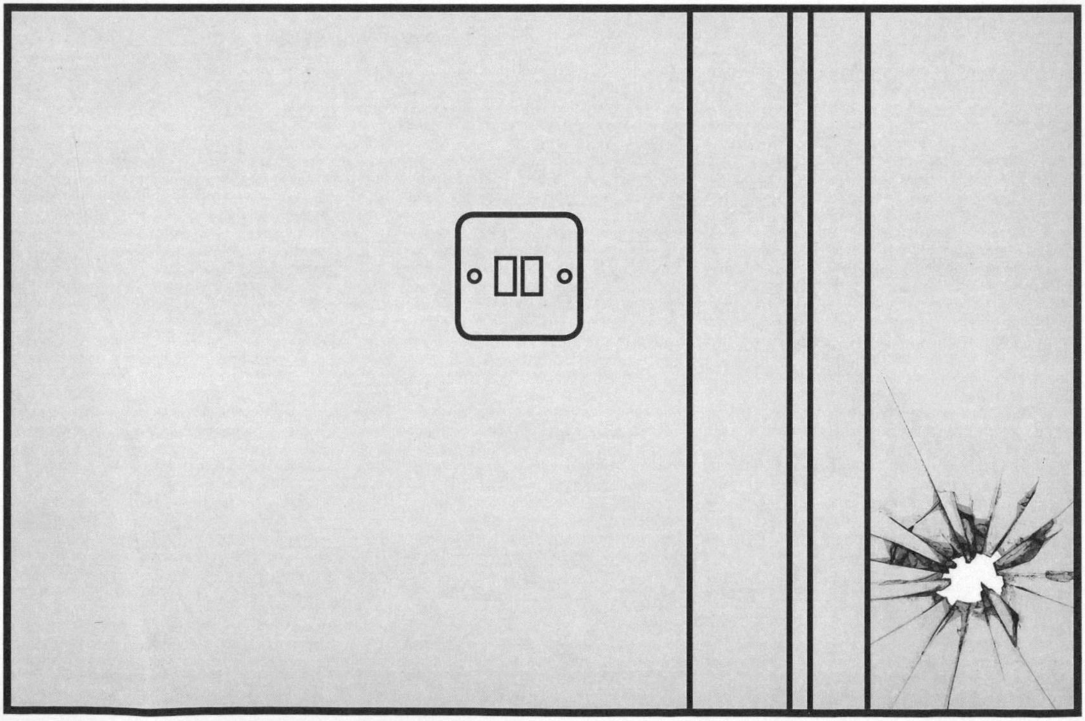